Eve Lockett is a licensed lay minister in the Diocese of Oxford. She regularly contributes to family services and for some years helped with an after-school club involving biblical storytelling. She is a volunteer for the Volunteer Reading Help scheme in her local primary school and enjoys sharing her love of children's books. Eve graduated in English and Fine Art from Exeter University, and has a diploma in Biblical and Theological Studies from Wycliffe Hall, Oxford. Her first book for BRF, *Tales of Grace*, was published in May 2005.

I c D. Ɑ

Text copyright © Eve Lockett 2007
The author asserts the moral right
to be identified as the author of this work

Published by
The Bible Reading Fellowship
First Floor, Elsfield Hall
15–17 Elsfield Way, Oxford OX2 8FG
Website: www.brf.org.uk

ISBN 978 1 84101 509 5
First published 2007
10 9 8 7 6 5 4 3 2 1 0
All rights reserved

Acknowledgments
Unless otherwise stated, scripture quotations taken from the
Contemporary English Version of the Bible, published by HarperCollins
Publishers, are copyright © 1991, 1992, 1995 American Bible Society.

The prayer 'Lighten our darkness, Lord we pray' from *Common Worship:
Services and Prayers for the Church of England* (Church House Publishing,
2000) is copyright © The Archbishops' Council 2000 and is reproduced
by permission.

A catalogue record for this book is available from the British Library

Printed in Singapore by Craft Print International Ltd

TALES
for the
Prayer Journey

30 five-minute stories
for all-age reflection and discussion,
with Bible links

Eve Lockett

For Miriam, Alice and Greta

ACKNOWLEDGMENTS

I would like to thank the following people for sharing with me their thoughts on prayer. I appreciated their wisdom, their stories, their encouragement and enthusiasm. They are: members of Cumnor Parish young people's group JAM, Richard and Helene Schwier, Sally Spicer and Chrissie Wilkinson.

I would also like to thank Jenny Hyson for her time and advice. And again, my thanks to my husband David for his love, patience, encouragement and interest.

CONTENTS

FOREWORD

Thank-you juice for rusty bicycles, cantankerous crabs, quiet giants, lentil, ginger and chocolate pancakes, a young girl kidnapped by pirates, a rabbit who throws the best parties in town and a letter from a boy in Galilee who has just seen Jesus—they are all here in this kaleidoscope of stories from Eve Lockett. It's a treasure trove of adventure and reflection that children will enjoy and, through the helpful accompanying notes, they will be enabled to go deeper in their own relationship with God.

Many parents find it hard to pray with their children or talk with them about the Christian faith. This book will help enormously. It can also be used in church and in school to explore the ongoing dialogue of Christian spirituality, for these are stories for a prayer journey—tales that can be enjoyed on their own terms but can also be used to raise all sorts of issues and questions about how we develop and sustain a lifelong conversation with God.

Children are good at prayer. They have a natural sense of wonder and an inbuilt thankfulness. They love to enquire and create. The world—and, too often, the church—knocks that out of them. These stories will help keep it in place, building foundations for a prayerful life—and the adults will also be blessed. Let us not forget that Jesus himself taught us through stories.

The Right Revd Stephen Cottrell, Bishop of Reading

⁘

INTRODUCTION

Those who pray have a wonderful resource to help them in a difficult, confusing and dangerous world. Prayer brings us into the company of God. It is adventurous, energizing, intimate, healing. To introduce children to prayer, or to help them deepen their prayer life, is to equip them in a very special way.

And yet, talking to children about prayer, and praying with children, is challenging. For many adults—parents and carers, teachers, children's work leaders and clergy—talking about prayer with children means facing very difficult questions. 'What words should I use? What if it doesn't work? Why does God answer some prayers and not others? How do we know if it's God's will?'

There are other challenges facing adults as well. For example, what do we do if children persist in believing that God will do something in situations where we adults would exercise more caution? Again, it is sometimes difficult for us as adults to cope with children praying more naturally and honestly than we do. It is difficult to teach about prayer when we feel we are the ones who need to learn.

The purpose of this book is to engage children *and* adults on a journey where both learn about prayer together. It is not a book of instructions on how to pray; nor does it give watertight answers to all those difficult questions. It is intended to encourage discussion and reflection on prayer itself; to help us grow in our prayer life.

HOW TO USE THIS BOOK

Tales for the Prayer Journey contains ten principal themes on the subject of prayer, with each explored in three chapters looking at the theme from different angles. Themes include the importance of listening to God, being honest with God, trusting God and waiting for his kingdom. A short introduction to each chapter explains how it relates to our own prayer life and gives examples from the Bible.

Each chapter contains a five-minute story. The story can be read aloud or told in one's own words, in a group of adults, a group of children or a mixed group of adults and children. Equally, the story can be used for personal reflection and read to oneself. Stories are a way of illustrating and exploring truths whilst allowing us to reach our own conclusions. The story is intended as an introduction to promote reflection, discussion and further Bible study.

The story is followed by suggestions for prayer steps, using visual aids, Bible stories and activities. The prayer steps are offered as an aid to deepen an ongoing prayer life, for children as well as adults, and the hope is that adults will use the material to reflect on their own prayer life and as a guide for children.

Four Bible passages have been chosen to go with each theme. The accompanying questions are given as an aid to reflection, Bible study and discussion. Some or all of these references can be used with children, along with the key verse in each chapter.

Suggestions are made for adults and children to pray on their own or in a group. Group activities may take the form of a discussion or game or a drama to help illustrate the theme.

Finally, there is a written prayer offered in two versions so that it can be used as a model for private prayer or said at the end of a group session.

USING A PRAYER JOURNAL

Some people find it very rewarding to keep a prayer journal. It doesn't have to be a daily diary; it can be written at the end of the week or from time to time as you feel you want to record some thoughts for prayer or reflection. It is also a place for writing in any answer to prayer that you feel God has given you or recording the way some situation has worked out. Include any Bible verses that strike you and anything you feel God is teaching you or speaking to you about.

A prayer journal is a good place to keep photographs as a reminder to pray, letters from people with specific needs or news, and any pictures that speak to you on a special subject. Children can enjoy making their own prayer journal, decorating the cover, making a bookmark for it and writing down their prayers and thoughts.

GRUMPY OR GRACIOUS: BEING HONEST WITH GOD

> **Jonah was really upset and angry. So he prayed…**
> JONAH 4:1–2

INTRODUCTION

Sometimes we think we have to put on a nice smile and sound very polite when we pray. That isn't how people prayed in the Bible. They came to God even when they were angry or upset or confused, and they didn't pretend everything was all right. Jonah was angry with God for blessing his enemies. Mary of Bethany was upset with Jesus because he had not saved her brother's life. Peter was confused that God had asked him to do something he thought was wrong.

If we are honest with God when something upsets us, we often find a better way to deal with it.

 THE MIRROR

Prince Julian drew his cloak around him and stood upright. 'Thank you for joining me today, my friends,' he said. 'In a week I shall be king, and I shall not forget you.'

The people gathered around him smiled and bowed and looked grateful. Julian bowed in turn and then left the room. Instead of going down the carpeted hallway to his own room, he walked along the corridors until he came to a quieter part of the castle. There he breathed a sigh of relief, grateful to be alone. As he reached the door to one of the turrets, he noticed an old silver mirror hanging on the wall. Julian paused and gazed at himself in the mirror's surface. 'I shall be king,' he said, and he tried to look stately and proud, but all he saw was the face of a boy. He practised looking stern and gracious at the same time, but instead he looked rather silly. Annoyed, he tried again. 'An important person, noble, brave, with an air of command,' he told himself, but the mirror showed none of these.

'In a week I shall be king!' cried Julian out loud. 'Mirror, I command you to show me as I am.'

A ripple seemed to go over the surface of the mirror, and the boy's face looked, if anything, younger.

Julian heard people coming down the corridor and he ducked through the turret door. When they had passed by, he came out and looked again in the mirror. This time he made a huge effort to appear older, wiser and more powerful. The ripple happened again, and the prince had the strangest impression that the mirror was laughing. He began to get seriously angry. Taking off his cloak, he threw it over the mirror's surface and then went downstairs to eat his dinner.

The next few days, the prince kept thinking about the mirror, wanting to remove the cloak. But it was not till the night before his coronation, as he was walking to and fro in his bedroom, that he made up his mind to take one more look. 'I must appear like a king now,' he thought. Going along the darkened corridor, he lifted a torch from its bracket and carried it over to the mirror.

Removing the cloak, Julian gazed again at his reflection. What he saw made him cry out in dismay. 'No!' he cried angrily. 'Why do you mock me like this?'

'I do not mock,' said a silvery voice. 'I show what I see. I cannot do anything else.'

Wondering at the voice, the prince looked around him, not quite believing it could have come from the mirror.

The voice went on: 'If you pretend with me, I will show you pretending. Many, many people at your court have stood where you stand. And nearly all of them were pretending to be happy or good or clever. But I am your friend, prince, whereas many people are false.'

'You are no friend. Why do you show me like that? As a... a... frightened child?'

The prince turned and ran back down the corridor to his room. But he could not sleep. He knew that the face he had seen was truly his own.

In the early hours of the morning Julian crept back, quiet and pale, and lifted his face to the mirror. When he spoke, he sounded sad and shaken.

'It's no use, mirror. The truth is that I am afraid. I cannot tell my friends from my foes. So much depends on a king's wisdom and strength. I have a king's crown waiting for me, but I am afraid to wear it.'

'You have begun to wear it already,' said the mirror. 'You have begun by being true.'

And as Julian stood before his reflection, his own eyes looked back at him—eyes that were clear and steady and shone from the heart of a king.

PRAYER STEPS

Praying with a visual aid

Have available some shaving or make-up mirrors. Alone or in a group, look at your image in both sides of the mirror. Follow with a time of personal reflection or shared discussion. How do you feel about the two images? Which of the images do you like better? Which one do you feel is the better likeness?

Praying with the Bible

Use the following passages for personal reflection or discussion.

* **Genesis 17:17–19; 18:10–15:** Abraham laughed when God promised him a son. The name Isaac means 'laughter'. Did Sarah's laughter matter? Was it worse that she lied?
* **Jonah 4:1–11:** Why was Jonah angry with God? Was God provoking Jonah to be more angry? How was he teaching him a lesson?
* **John 11:32–37:** Mary met Jesus with an accusation. How did he react to her accusation and to her grief? Do we voice our true feelings in our prayers?
* **Acts 11:1–18:** What was Peter's first response to the vision? How did God use Peter's natural feelings to teach him something? Do we trust God with our honest responses?

Praying on your own

Quietly reflect on how we enter into prayer. Instead of rushing into prayer, how can we take time to be still and to be honest with ourselves and with God? When we pray, are we hiding or pretending at all?

Praying in a group

Draw some blank faces. Draw different expressions on them, for example sad, happy, angry, frightened, unkind or bored. Pin them up around the room. Think about which face shows how you are feeling right now. Say a prayer like the one written below.

Praying it through

Draw your thoughts together in a time of quiet reflection, or use the appropriate version of the prayer below.

Lord, help me to be honest with you. However I am feeling, draw me closer to you. Amen

Lord, help us to be honest with you. However we are feeling, draw us closer to you. Amen

✛

TOO YOUNG?: PRAYER IS NOT JUST FOR ADULTS

> **'Don't you hear what those children are saying?'**
> MATTHEW 21:16

INTRODUCTION

You might think that older people know how to pray better than you do. But we have a lot to learn about prayer from each other, whatever our age.

The Bible shows us that we are never too young to worship and obey God.

Josiah was only eight years old when he became king, and when he was still very young he taught people to follow God in the right way. Some people were angry that children were praising Jesus in the temple, but Jesus told them that God intended children to praise him.

 TWITCHERS

'Don't bother me, Jack. I've just seen a reed bunting.'

Jack let go of his dad's pocket and kicked a loose stone across the path. He'd have liked to hurl it into the lake, but he knew his dad would go mad. So would all the other twitchers—the birdwatchers gathered around the water's edge. Someone walked past with a spaniel on a lead. Jack hoped the dog would race into the water, sending ducks and geese shrieking in all directions. But the dog looked far too well behaved to do anything of the sort.

The twitchers had their binoculars and telescopes trained on the far side, where some long-legged birds were dipping their beaks in and out of the water. 'Ah yes!' said his father. 'Black-tailed godwits. And I believe there's a curlew among them. Yes, yes there it is!'

Jack was bored of birds. He wanted to get to the end of the path and out on to the beach, but his dad was taking ages. Two girls came by, both about Jack's age. They had binoculars around their necks, and their parents were pointing to the water's edge. One of the girls opened a bird book and looked through the pages. 'Here it is,' she said. 'It's a redshank.'

'Well done!' said their mother.

Jack was surprised any children were birdwatching. His dad had never offered to buy him a pair of binoculars. 'You can look through mine if you want to,' his dad had told him. 'When you show any real interest, I might get you some.' But whenever Jack's dad saw a really unusual bird, he was too excited to let Jack take a look.

Jack went off by himself and found a wooden bench by the pathway. He noticed it had been donated in memory of 'Celia Barnes, aged 94, who loved to sit here and watch the lake'.

Jack sat down, trying to imagine that he was very old and loved birdwatching. He crouched forward slightly and raised one wavering hand to shield his eyes from the sun. Turning his head in a slow arc, from one side to the other, he rested his gaze on a clump of bushes by the lake. Everything suddenly seemed to go quiet, and for a moment Jack felt he and Celia were watching the lake together. A bird darted out and perched on a twig hanging over the water. Jack couldn't help thinking it was unusual. It had a blue patch on its chest, and in the middle of the blue patch was a round, red spot. 'It looks like a target,' thought Jack. He was about to call his dad to ask what it was when the bird flew back into the bush and disappeared. No one else had seen it.

'Come on,' called his dad. 'Let's get to the beach. The tide's on the turn, and there should be plenty to see.'

Later, as they wandered around the shop for birdwatchers, Jack picked up a copy of the same book the two girls had been holding. He flicked through the pages and noticed a picture of the strange bird he had seen.

'What's this, Dad?' he asked, holding out the page.

'That? That's a red-spotted bluethroat. Very rare to see one here.'

'Could I see one?' asked Jack.

His dad gave a laugh. 'Maybe. When you're older. If you're lucky.'

Jack pulled some money out of his pocket and, to his dad's surprise, handed the book over to the salesgirl. 'I'd like to buy this,' he said.

'What made you interested all of a sudden?' asked his father.

Jack answered softly, 'Celia Barnes.' But his dad was too far away to hear him.

PRAYER STEPS

Praying with a visual aid

On your own or in a group, trace the outline of your hand on to A4 card and cut out the shape. Use the image of hands as a focus for quiet reflection or shared discussion. How can we use our hands to help others? In what ways does the size or dexterity of our hands make a difference to what we can accomplish... on our own... or with others? In what ways can we use our hands in worship?

Praying with the Bible

Use the following passages for personal reflection or discussion.

* **2 Kings 5:1–10:** What qualities did the young Israelite girl demonstrate? How were her words received? Are young people listened to in your church?
* **2 Chronicles 34:1–3:** Josiah's father and grandfather were evil kings. How did this young boy honour God? What does the reference to his age teach us?
* **Matthew 21:14–17:** What was the objection of the leaders to the children? What was significant about the children's words? In what ways do adults acknowledge the faith of young people?
* **1 Timothy 4:11–16:** What ministry did Timothy have? What did he risk by being so young? In what ways do adults take young people seriously? When do adults think of following the example of young people?

Praying on your own

Read the verses from the psalm below and think about what they mean. Then read all or some of the lines out loud as a way of worshipping God.

Praying in a group

As a group, think of ways that praise and honour of God's name can be passed from generation to generation. The psalm below was written hundreds of years ago, but we can still use it in our worship. Try reading it 'antiphonally'. This means half your group say the first line, and the other half the second line, and so on. Then all say the last line together.

Praying it through

Draw your thoughts together using the prayer below.

I will praise you, my God and King, and always honour your name.
I will praise you each day and always honour your name.
You are wonderful, Lord, and you deserve all praise,
because you are much greater than anyone can understand...
You are merciful, Lord! You are kind and patient and always loving.
You are good to everyone, and you take care of all your creation...
I will praise you, Lord, and everyone will respect your holy name for ever.
PSALM 145:1–3, 8–9, 21

WHAT DO YOU WANT?: PRAYING OUR DEEPEST WISHES

> **You satisfy the desires of all your worshippers.**
> PSALM 145:19

INTRODUCTION

Sometimes we don't pray what we most want because we don't think God will be pleased. That's true if we want something that's wrong or unkind or greedy. But God may very well give us a deep wish that fulfils his purposes.

If we are not sure whether what we want is in God's will, it is still good to share with him what is on our hearts, because it brings us closer to him. Jesus taught his disciples to make sure that what they wanted most was God's kingdom. Naomi longed for children and grandchildren, and the grandchild born to her was one of the ancestors of Jesus. Paul longed to see his own people come to love Jesus and follow him. Jesus told his disciples that God was pleased to give them his kingdom.

 ## THE LAND BEYOND THE SEA

Eric pushed away a sheep that was grazing too near his foot, and gazed out over the sea. The air was heavy with the damp morning, and foam blew across the surface of the waves. The smell of the sea woke the deepest longing in him to be on a ship, sailing over the rim of the world, seeking adventure and exploring new lands.

The flock of sheep grazed steadily hour after hour as he kept watch. They were beginning to look scrawny, their fleeces straggly and thin. The grass, which should have covered the ground, was growing in clumps, too sparse to feed the hungry flock.

That evening, as he and his brothers sat on benches at the table, Eric found his thoughts returning to the sea. His mother turned from stirring the pot over the fire and pushed the hair out of her eyes.

'Dreaming as usual, Eric. Still dreaming of sailing away. What use would you be then? I'd be pleased to sail away myself, but there's not much chance of that. Not with all the family to feed.'

Grumbling, she slapped some bread on to the table in front of him and he took it before his brothers could reach for it.

His father came home late, looking worried. There'd been another council meeting. Times were bad, the villages were becoming too crowded, and the land could not grow enough food. Families were wandering away looking for a better living in other places. Some had come back, saying it was the same everywhere.

'Bjorn is talking about finding a new land,' his father reported. 'Way over the sea. He's looking for men to sail with him.'

'More widows, then,' said his mother. 'You never think of that, you men, when you have ideas.'

'Don't worry, no one looked keen to join him.'

Eric stopped breathing for a moment. If only he could go. If only he could stand on the wooden planks of a great ship, riding the waves of the sea.

The next evening, Eric slipped out of the house and followed his father. The meeting hall was in the centre of the village, and it was already crowded and noisy. Eric kept to one side and made his way round the back of the crowd. Bjorn was making a speech.

'Who will come?' he said in his deep voice. 'I do not order you to come. I offer you the chance to bring hope to your families, and to explore the mystery beyond the sea. Who will join me?'

'I will,' cried Eric, in a voice that carried high over their heads. 'I'll come with you!'

Faces turned towards him, and Eric realized what he'd done. All he could think was that his mother would be furious.

'Come forward, boy.' Eric pushed into the centre of the throng. Heat from the fire reached his face and legs, making them glow. Bjorn took his hand and held it up in the air.

'This boy is not afraid. Now will you come with me? Will you be shamed by a boy?'

Some men looked annoyed and some grinned, but one by one they stood forward.

'I'm proud of him,' Eric's father told his mother when they got home. 'He brings us all hope. A new land, with green hills for our sheep and good soil to grow wheat. A land where there is enough food for all of us. Isn't that what you want for our children?'

'Yes,' she replied simply. 'It is what I long for.'

PRAYER STEPS

Praying with a visual aid

Have available a jug of cold water and drinking glass(es). On your own or in a group, slowly fill the drinking glass(es) with water. Take a sip of the water and savour the taste and the feel of the liquid in your mouth. As you continue to slowly sip from the glass, reflect on your need for the life-sustaining gift of water. What good things in your life do you enjoy most? Follow with a time of personal reflection or shared discussion.

Praying with the Bible

Use the following passages for personal reflection or discussion.

* **Ruth 1:19–21; 4:13–17:** Who does Naomi blame for her loss? In what ways do the women see her as blessed?
* **Psalm 145:17–21:** What do these verses tell us about the Lord? How can we be sure our prayers are sincere?
* **Luke 12:32–34:** What is Jesus teaching his disciples about trust? How can their hearts be directed in the right way? What does Jesus mean by treasure?
* **Romans 10:1–4:** How does Paul regard the people of Israel? What does he long for them to understand?

Praying on your own

Take a piece of paper and write or draw something you most wish. If you don't know what it is yourself, then just draw a box and try to imagine what is inside it. Hold the piece of paper as you pray, using your own words or the prayer below.

God wants you, and all that makes up who you are, to belong to him and to be in his kingdom.

Praying in a group

Take a piece of paper and write or draw something you most wish. If you don't want anyone else to know, just draw a box with a lock on it. Hold the piece of paper as you pray, using your own words or the prayer below.

Praying it through

Draw your thoughts together in a time of quiet reflection, or use the appropriate version of the prayer below.

Father, you know all my deepest wishes. I come to you just as I am. I pray that you will help me to follow you with all my heart. Amen

Father, you know all our deepest wishes. We come to you just as we are. We pray that you will help us to follow you with all our hearts. Amen

THANK YOU!:
HAVING A GRATEFUL HEART

> **Be thankful and praise the Lord as you enter his temple.**
> PSALM 100:4

INTRODUCTION

Many people have found that saying 'thank you' to God can change the way we look at things. We can find God's blessing even in difficult or painful situations when we are ready to thank him for all his goodness.

In the Old Testament, David thanked God for all he was and for all he had done. Then David told all the people with him to thank and praise God as well. In Luke's Gospel, Jesus thanked his Father in heaven that ordinary people were responding to him, while some very important and powerful people were ignoring him. He could have grumbled about it! But he saw that God's plans were deeper and wiser than that.

 THANK-YOU JUICE

'It's a rubbish bike—it doesn't work,' said Ned. He put his feet on the ground and pushed the bike into the garage. 'It's even slow going downhill.'

Ned's grandpa looked up from his workbench. Ned's face was sour and cross.

'It's a good bike. It just hasn't been ridden for years. Here, let me see.'

Grandpa held the bike by the handlebars and the saddle and ran it backwards and forwards. 'It just needs some juice, that's all.'

'Juice? What good is juice?' Ned started kicking pebbles against a tin box full of tools.

'This is special juice.' Grandpa reached up to the top shelf of his garage and took down a large red oilcan. Then he took a tin of oil and poured some of it into the oilcan.

'That's oil,' said Ned. 'Why do you call it juice?'

'It's thank-you juice.' Grandpa tilted the can and peered inside at the yellow liquid. 'When I oil a bit of machinery, I always hear it say "thank you". I can feel how grateful it is. Being grateful is good for machines. It's good for people, too.'

Ned snorted. He didn't want to be with his grandpa, he wanted to be at home with his friends. But his mother was in hospital and Grandpa had said he could stay for a while. Ned was bored and anxious and cross.

'Come on,' said Grandpa. 'You can help me. You'll see the difference.'

Ned held the handlebars, and Grandpa unscrewed the top of the bell. He dribbled some oil into the bell's workings and then pulled the lever back. The bell gave a gurgle. Grandpa screwed the lid back on and tried again.

'There,' he said. 'Can you hear that? It's saying "thank you, thank you".'

'It's just ringing,' grumbled Ned.

'You need to listen properly. But you're right. It's no good just making thank-you noises. You have to have a "thank you" deep inside for it to do any good. What shall we try next?'

'The chain?' Ned suggested.

'Ah. Right to the heart of it. Yes, the chain.'

They tipped the bike upside down, and Ned wound the pedals round while Grandpa dripped oil on to the chain. There was a moment when Ned thought he really did hear the whirring chain say 'thank you, thank you'. He glanced up at his grandpa.

'You heard it?' said Grandpa. 'Next, the pedals.'

They oiled the pedals and the wheels, till both spun freely. 'Lastly, the saddle,' said Grandpa. 'It's a bit high for you, so let me lower it a bit.'

He oiled the saddle and wrenched it from side to side. 'Thank you, thank you,' said the saddle and settled in to its new position.

Grandpa held the bike out to his grandson. 'There you go, Ned. Try that.'

Ned took the bike out on to the path and he sensed the wheels spinning smoothly beneath him. Sweeping along, he began to feel happy and free. He turned and rode back past the garage where his grandfather was working. Ned rang the bell. 'Thank you, thank you,' called the bell.

Grandpa lifted a hand and waved. 'My pleasure, Ned,' he called back. 'Come in when you're ready, and we'll have a cup of tea. That's *my* thank-you juice.'

PRAYER STEPS

Praying with a visual aid

Find or make a 'thank you' card. As a group or on your own, take a moment just to look at it. Imagine receiving the card. What might people be thanking you for? What does it feel like to be thanked? Imagine sending the card. Who would you send it to and what would you say? What does it feel like to be thanking someone else? Follow with a time of personal reflection or shared discussion.

Praying with the Bible

Use the following passages for personal reflection or discussion.

* **1 Chronicles 29:10–20:** Pick out all the things for which David praises and thanks God. What does he pray about himself and the people? How can we use this prayer as a pattern for our prayers?
* **Psalm 100:** What reasons are given for the people to rejoice? Is this how we feel as we go to church? Is it possible to be thankful even when we are distressed or suffering? In what ways do we feel pressure to show a false cheerfulness?
* **Luke 10:21–24:** For what is Jesus thanking his Father in heaven? How have the disciples been blessed? Do you find that joy and thankfulness go together?
* **Philippians 4:4–7:** What is a thankful heart? Is it more than saying 'thank you' for something? What outcome is promised for those who give thanks and pray?

Praying on your own

Imagine you've been oiled with thank-you juice. For what sort of things do you want to say thank you to God?

Praying in a group

Put together a thank-you prayer to God. Invite each person to think of one thing to thank God for, and then put them all together, like a psalm. You could use verses from Psalm 100 at the beginning and end.

Praying it through

Draw your thoughts together in a time of quiet reflection, or use the appropriate version of the prayer below.

Thank you, Lord, that in sad times and in good times, in difficult times and in happy times, your love is still the same and you are still with me. Amen

Thank you, Lord, that in sad times and in good times, in difficult times and in happy times, your love is still the same and you are still with us. Amen

✦

SAYING SORRY:
ADMITTING WHEN WE HAVE
DONE SOMETHING WRONG

> **'I'll tell the Lord each one of my sins.'**
> PSALM 32:5

INTRODUCTION

Telling God when we have done something wrong is important. It can also be painful. It makes us feel less proud of ourselves than we would like to be. But God encourages us to tell him. If we are truly sorry, he promises to forgive us.

In Psalm 32, God forgives those who do not hide what they've done wrong, but tell him. In the Gospels, John the Baptist told people to confess all they had done wrong to God, and then he baptized them in the river, to show they were now clean from their sins. Someone else called John wrote to the early church, saying that if we confess our sins to God, he will forgive us, because Jesus died to take our sins away.

 ## CRAB LEGS

'Ha ha ha!' laughed Barney. He was laughing at Lucy who had only nine legs. She'd had ten, like the other crabs, but one had been bitten off by a fat green fish.

Barney was being unkind. He was in a bad mood because the school term had started and he was still thinking about the holidays. Their teacher, Mr Pinch, came into the cave. Mr Pinch was a huge crab and very old. His shell was chipped and scratched in several places. But he was extremely strong, and when he wanted to move, he was faster than any of them.

'Maths!' cried Mr Pinch. 'Ten plus ten.'

'Twenty,' called out a clever crab.

Barney couldn't help it—he whispered, 'Or nineteen, if you're Lucy.'

His friend Claude tried not to giggle and just blew bubbles instead. Mr Pinch looked at them. He had very good eyesight. But he said nothing. As the day went on, Barney cheered up. He was enjoying his favourite subject—eating. It wasn't that simple: the young crabs had to learn what was food and what wasn't. Where to find it. How to catch it. How not to end up as someone else's food. How to pretend to be a stone or a shell or hide in the seaweed.

'Well done!' Mr Pinch said to him, as Barney pounced on a tiny shellfish. 'You're good at this.'

Barney glowed, and gobbled the shellfish.

'Keep still,' hissed Mr Pinch suddenly. A dark shape glided through the water above their heads. Barney could feel the water shaking around him, and he froze like a stone. He felt sure the fish would notice him. He had never been so scared. At last, very slowly, the fish swam away, and they all relaxed.

Barney noticed Lucy was quivering like a jellyfish. 'You're safe now,' said Mr Pinch kindly. 'Come on, back to the cave.'

Barney felt rather sorry he'd laughed at Lucy. The fish had

been very frightening. But he didn't like feeling sorry, so he pretended not to care.

The next day, Lucy was not at school. Barney felt worse. By the end of the second day he knew he had to find out.

'Is Lucy all right?' he asked Mr Pinch, when no one was listening. Mr Pinch gave him a very straight stare. He knows, thought Barney, and took a deep breath. 'I wasn't kind to her,' he confessed. 'I laughed at her leg.'

'Lucy is fine,' said Mr Pinch. 'She'll be back tomorrow. You won't laugh at her any more.'

'No,' said Barney. 'Sorry.'

The next morning, Lucy came back to school. Something had happened to her. She had grown a new shell. She was larger than before—and she had ten legs. 'My old shell fell off,' she told her friends. 'My leg grew back with my new shell.'

Barney felt a bit nervous of her now she was bigger than him. He tried to avoid her, but she wouldn't let him. 'That was a big fish, wasn't it?' she said to him. 'Were you scared?'

'Yes,' said Barney, truthfully, and then he added, 'Was it bigger than the other fish? The one that bit your leg off?'

'That one was enormous,' said Lucy. 'Do you want to hear about it?'

'Yes, please!' said Barney.

'Yes, please!' said all the other crabs, and they settled down to listen.

PRAYER STEPS

Praying with a visual aid

Gather together some objects that are chipped or broken. Include a torn page or picture, torn cloth, and something spoilt by scribbles. Then put together a repair kit of sellotape, glue, correcting fluid, eraser, needle and thread, and whatever else you can think of. On your own or in a group, set about repairing some of the objects. Take time to reflect on or discuss what you have done. Why do we need to repair so many things? What does it feel like to repair something? What are the ways we can repair things in ourselves, in society and in our relationships?

Praying with the Bible

Use the following passages for personal reflection or discussion.

* ✶ **2 Chronicles 6:36–39**: What is Solomon asking God on behalf of the people? How are the people to feel and act before God forgives them? What is the significance of the temple?
* ✶ **Psalm 32**: What does this psalm teach us about God's nature? What does it teach us about the way to live in relationship with God? Who are the righteous and good?
* ✶ **Matthew 3:1–6**: What was John's message? What were the people saying about themselves by being baptized? Are we ready for God's kingdom?
* ✶ **1 John 1:6–10**: What is meant by the light and the dark? What are the signs of living in the light? Why are we to confess our sins? What is the significance of the blood of Jesus?

Praying on your own

Ask yourself if there is something you have done that makes you feel bad. Tell God about it, just as you would tell a friend. In your Bible, look up 1 John 1:9, and you will see God's promise to forgive you.

Praying in a group

Get ready a towel and a plastic bowl of water. Take a while to think of things you have done wrong, such as being unkind, selfish, lazy, telling lies, stealing, being in a bad mood. Say a prayer together, such as the prayer written below, telling God you are sorry. During the prayer time, you may like to dip your hands in the water and then dry them, as a symbol of God's washing those things away.

Praying it through

Draw your thoughts together in a time of quiet reflection, or use the appropriate version of the prayer below.

Dear Lord, I am sorry I do things to hurt you and other people. I ask you to forgive me and keep me from doing the same things again. Amen

Dear Lord, we are sorry we do things to hurt you and other people. We ask you to forgive us and keep us from doing the same things again. Amen

YOU AND ME:
PRAYING FOR OTHER PEOPLE

> **While Peter was being kept in jail, the church never stopped praying to God for him.**
> ACTS 12:5

INTRODUCTION

Prayer isn't just about praying for ourselves or for what we want. Praying is a way of caring for other people, and realizing how God cares for them.

In the Old Testament, Nehemiah prayed for God's help for himself, his family and all the people of Israel. In the Gospels, some friends of a man who couldn't walk were so determined to bring him to Jesus they took the roof to pieces to get him inside the house. In the same way, in our prayers we can bring our friends to Jesus. In the book of Acts, Peter was set free from jail while the disciples were praying for him. They were very surprised to see him! God may answer our prayers in ways we don't expect.

 TRUFFLE THE BADGER

On the edge of Bessie's wood was a large quarry, where men came with great digging machines and took away lorryloads of yellow stone. Around the edge of the quarry they had put up stakes and a barbed-wire fence to keep out any intruders.

The badgers did not normally come out so far into the open, but Truffle was too busy hunting to notice how close he had come to the fence. He was snuffling in the grass for worms and beetles and had just found a very tasty caterpillar when he felt a sudden pain in the back of his neck. Something sharp was sticking into his fur.

Truffle jerked back and another pain darted through his leg, high up near his shoulder. He twisted round, trying to run away, and felt a tight pain around his throat and under his tummy. Whichever way he pulled made the pain worse. He whimpered and kept still, wondering what to do.

The sun was beginning to glow along the edge of the woods, and Truffle knew that soon the men would come back to work in the quarry. People also walked their dogs across the open ground. He was afraid of what they would do if they found him. He struggled and pulled, trying to ignore the pain, but the wire held him fast. Truffle longed to be back home, running into the sett, to the warmth of the earth and the other badgers.

'Truffle!' cried a squeaky voice. 'What's happened? What are you doing here?'

It was Frog, his little brother, bounding all round him as usual. 'Wow! You're caught in the wire! I can see blood.'

'I'm stuck.' Truffle raised his eyes sadly. 'I can't move. You'd better go home before anyone comes with their dogs.'

'I'll get help,' promised Frog, beginning to run. 'Stay there!'

Frog found his cousins Mint and Stinkie fighting each other. He dived on top of them, growling. 'Listen!' he said. 'Truffle is trapped in barbed wire and he's bleeding.'

'What can we do?' they said to each other. 'We need help. Who can we ask?'

They asked Grandfather badger, who looked very worried. They asked Truffle's mother, who ran round in a circle, crying.

'This is getting us nowhere,' complained Frog.

'We'll have to do something fast,' said Stinkie.

Mint looked thoughtful for a while. Then she started running away through the trees. 'I've got an idea,' she called back to them. 'Come on!'

That night as the young badgers returned to their sett, Truffle was with them. He crawled inside, and lay there licking his wounds. The older badgers gathered around, anxious to know what had happened.

'We went to see that woman who lives in the caravan,' said Mint. 'The one who's always feeding us. We scratched and scratched on her door till she had to open it. She followed us to the quarry. Then we saw her talking to one of the men.'

Truffle carried on the story. 'The man came up from the quarry. But he didn't hurt me; he wanted to help. He got some pliers and cut the wire all round me. I was so frightened, I tried to bite and scratch him, but the wire stopped me. I pulled the rest of it out with my teeth. Then I ran away.'

'She's a good woman,' said Grandfather badger. 'But who'd have believed one of those men would have helped you?'

'She called him an angel,' said Mint. 'She said, "You're an angel, Tom." I heard her.'

'I think she's the angel,' said Truffle's mother. 'Which is more than you are, Truffle. Don't you ever do that again!'

But Truffle was asleep, and the only answer he gave her was a gentle snore.

PRAYER STEPS

Praying with a visual aid

Take a collection of Scrabble letters. Alone or as a group pick out one letter. Think of someone you know whose name begins with the same letter. Pick another letter and think of another person. Go on picking letters for a while. The people you choose could be friends, relatives, someone from school or work, or someone in the news. What are their stories? Do you notice how different they are from each other? How would you pray for them? Follow with a time of personal reflection or shared discussion.

Praying with the Bible

Use the following passages for personal reflection or discussion.

✳ **Nehemiah 1:5–11:** Who is Nehemiah praying for? What is he admitting they have done wrong? Why does he believe God will hear his prayers?

✳ **Luke 5:17–26:** Who are the different characters in this story? What is Jesus declaring about himself? What did the persistence of the man's friends show about them?

✳ **Acts 12:1–19:** What happened to James? What did the other disciples do while Peter was in prison? What did they think would happen to Peter? Why did they call Rhoda mad?

✳ **Colossians 4:2–4:** Paul asks the Colossians to pray for him. How does he say they should pray? What is he asking them to pray for? What does he see as most important?

Praying on your own

Think of someone you can pray for today. You might like to pray that God will be with them, and that they won't be afraid. Ask God to help them.

Praying in a group

Read the story of Peter in prison (Acts 12:1–19). You could act out the story or tell it as if you were one of the characters. Think about the way their feelings changed during the story. What difference do you think their prayers made?

Praying it through

Draw your thoughts together in a time of quiet reflection, or use the appropriate version of the prayer below.

Dear Lord, I pray that you will be close to anyone who is in pain, who is frightened, or who needs my prayers. I pray for (name...) today. Amen

Dear Lord, we pray that you will be close to anyone who is in pain, who is frightened, or who needs our prayers. We pray for (name...) today. Amen

SSSH!:
LISTENING TO GOD

INTRODUCTION

Talking to God is very important, but we need to listen as well. God may speak words into our minds or remind us of something in the Bible. We can also hear God through our conscience or in someone else's words to us. Listening to God is more than just hearing him speak. It means having a heart willing to do what he wants.

In the Old Testament, Samuel listened to God and asked God to show him what to do. In Luke's Gospel, Mary of Bethany listened to Jesus while he was teaching his disciples, and he said that she had made a good choice. In his letter, James tells us that it's no good listening unless we do what we've heard.

 ## THE QUIETEST GIANT

Once there was an old giant called Boot. He lived in a huge castle, and he had an enormous family. There were boy giants and girl giants, older giants and younger giants, children giants and grandchildren giants. And they were all very, very huge and very, very loud. Except one. One giant was very, very quiet. She was so quiet that the other giants never heard her speak at all, and they thought she couldn't say anything.

In one room of the castle was a large iron chest. It was locked with a large padlock, and the key was hidden. All giant Boot's treasure was kept in that chest. Without it, the giants would soon have run out of things to eat and money for clothes and shoes, and they would have had to leave the castle.

Now giant Boot grew very old and very weak, and he took to his bed. The other giants were very sad; they knew that he did not have long to live. One day Boot called all his family around his bedside to say goodbye. They came thumping up the stairs, calling to each other, and some of them were crying very, very loudly. The noise in the room was deafening. The old giant raised himself on one elbow.

'I have something to tell you,' he yelled. 'About the key to my treasure chest.' When they heard this, all the giants tried to keep quiet.

'Yes?' asked one of them. 'Where is the key?'

And they all started shouting the same question, 'Where's the key, where's the key?'

'Quiet!' shouted Boot as loudly as he could. They all paused for a second. 'I've told one of you where the key is,' he said. 'Only one of you knows.' And with that he fell back on his pillow and died.

The giants began to cry and call out and stomp about the room. Then they slowly left the room, one by one, and went to their bedrooms to have a good cry on their own.

Some time later they started discussing what Boot had told them. 'Do you know where the key is?' they asked each other. 'It's you, isn't it?' And they began to shout and quarrel among themselves.

'It's me,' said the quietest giant. 'I know where it is.' But none of the other giants heard her, because they were being so noisy. At last they were all exhausted and miserable and sat around on the floor and began to doze off. 'It's me,' said the quietest giant again. 'I know where the key is.'

Immediately all the giants woke up and started shouting at her. 'Where is it? How do you know? Why did he tell you? Speak up, where's the key?' She tried to tell them but again she had to wait until they were very quiet before she could be heard.

'I was going to tell you,' said the quietest giant. 'You go on to the roof…'

'Come back!' roared one of the giants to his brother who had started up the stairs.

'You go on to the roof,' said the quietest giant. 'And you'll find a telescope. If you look through the telescope, you'll see a tree. In the tree, there's a nesting box. The key is in the nesting box.'

After a massive crashing and thumping about, all the giants had gone up to the roof, down again, out into the garden, and shaken the tree until the nesting box had fallen down. Inside, there was the key to the treasure chest. 'Hurray!' they shouted. 'We've found it! We're all right now! We can stay in the castle.'

'Why did giant Boot tell you where the key was?' asked the oldest giant. And then he shouted, 'BE QUIET!' as loud as he could, so that he could hear the answer. All the other giants gradually quietened down as they waited for the quietest giant to speak.

'He told me,' began the quietest giant shyly, 'he told me because he said I was the only one who would listen.'

And she picked up the key from the ground and went back into the castle.

PRAYER STEPS

Praying with a visual aid

Set an alarm clock or kitchen clock to go off in three to five minutes. Place it so that you can't see its face. Alone or in a group, listen to the ticking until the alarm sounds. Did it seem a very long time to wait? Did the ticking appear softer and louder at times? Were you distracted by other noises? What did it feel like being silent for so long? Follow with a time of personal reflection or shared discussion.

Praying with the Bible

Use the following passages for personal reflection or discussion.

* ✷ **1 Samuel 3:1–10:** What can we learn from Samuel's response to Eli and to the Lord? Do you know people who have heard the Lord calling them? In what way?
* ✷ **Ecclesiastes 5:1–3:** Do we spend time listening to God when we enter a church? Do we prepare our hearts even before we get there? Are we good at thinking before we speak?
* ✷ **Luke 10:38–42:** What state was Martha in? What was Mary doing? Was she being lazy? How can we sit at Jesus' feet today and listen to him?
* ✷ **James 1:22–25:** What does James say about listening and not responding? How can we become better listeners to God's word?

Praying on your own

Listen to all the noises around you: the noises as far away as possible; then the closest noises. Listen to the thoughts in your head. Then try to listen to the silence in between the noises. Then begin to pray. The prayer below may help you.

Praying in a group

Play a music CD while you chatter or move around. Then gradually turn down the volume. Try to hear the noise as it gets fainter and fainter. You will all have to be very quiet and still so that you can go on hearing it as long as possible.

Praying it through

Draw your thoughts together in a time of quiet reflection, or use the appropriate version of the prayer below.

Lord, help me to listen to you. Help me to hear you even when it's very noisy. Help me to be willing to do what you say. Amen

Lord, help us to listen to you. Help us to hear you even when it's very noisy. Help us to be willing to do what you say. Amen

SHALL I?: PRAYING OUT LOUD IN A GROUP

> **'I can never think of what to say.'**
> EXODUS 4:10

INTRODUCTION

In some groups, people pray aloud in turn, or they pray aloud when they have something to say. Do you feel that if you don't take a turn to pray aloud, you aren't praying? Or would you like to pray aloud, but feel too nervous in case you say the wrong thing? If a group is praying, it's good to pray together for the same thing. Then you can say 'amen' when you agree to it. But that doesn't mean everyone has to pray aloud for God to hear them.

In the Old Testament, Moses didn't feel he was good at speaking. God reminded Moses that he would give him the words to say. But because Moses was still nervous, God sent his brother Aaron to help him. In Mark's Gospel, some people brought a man, who was deaf and couldn't talk, to Jesus for him to heal. We don't know how many of the people spoke aloud to Jesus, but whoever did spoke on behalf of all of them, including the deaf man. In the book of Acts, the disciples prayed a prayer together. We are not told which one of them spoke it or made it up; it is given as the prayer of all of them. After their prayer, the Holy Spirit gave them courage to speak about Jesus.

ASKING MR FURBANK

'You go first.'

'No, you.'

'You ask him.'

'No, you.'

'I'm not asking him. He's fierce. Berry can ask him.'

'I'm not asking him. It was your idea.'

The six mice crowded under the floorboards, squeaking and twitching their whiskers. Their names were Lime, Berry, Breadcrumb, Pickle, Hazelnut and String. Their mother had named them after all the things she'd eaten just after they were born.

As they argued, they moved nearer and nearer to the hole in the side of the shed, until one by one they tumbled out into the moonlight. Quickly, they scuttled across the path and hid together under the holly bush.

'I don't mind asking him,' said Pickle. 'But I'm not going on my own. They say he's got very sharp teeth.'

'We can all ask him at the same time,' said Hazelnut.

Lime nodded. He knew he would be too nervous to say anything. He was always too nervous to say anything. But he could still nod.

Berry led the way across the garden to the fence. They followed her as she climbed over into the neighbouring garden. A large ginger cat watched them from an upstairs window, scratching to get out. Its owner was sound asleep, and the cat soon gave up and snuggled into the folds of the duvet.

The mice climbed out through a hedge and then crossed a

piece of open ground down to the river. Built on the side of the river was a small wooden jetty. The mice ran under the planks of the jetty and started calling out. 'Mr Furbank. Mr Furbank!'

A very whiskery vole pushed his nose out of the reeds. When the mice saw him, they fell silent and kept very still.

'Yes?' he asked in a sort of grunt.

'Er...' Pickle found he'd forgotten what he was going to say. All he could think about was Mr Furbank's sharp teeth.

'Mr Furbank,' said Breadcrumb and Hazelnut, speaking together very quickly. 'We're a family of mice. We've come a long way to see you. We've come to ask ...er.'

'Yes?' said the water vole again. 'What do you want me to do?'

Lime was nodding hard. The vole turned to look at him, and something strange happened. Lime felt less nervous than he normally did. 'Have you seen the riverboat?' he asked.

Pickle explained. 'Our uncle Silas travels on it. We want to join him. Our mum has had six new children and now she's going to have some more, and there isn't room for us all in the same garden. We'd like to go on the river.' All the mice nodded and squeaked, all except String.

'What about you?' the vole asked him.

String sniffed. 'I get seasick,' he said.

'I have seen the riverboat,' Mr Furbank told them. 'I see it every day. It goes downstream in the morning and then comes back upstream in the evening. Is that what you wanted to know?'

'Will you take a message for us?' asked Berry. 'Just to say we're here, and can we join him?'

'Yes, I will,' said the water vole. 'You may have to wait a long time for an answer.'

The mice were so excited they said they didn't mind waiting. But it was two days before they saw Mr Furbank again. Uncle Silas had a reply for them. They could join him until they found a new place to live. But seven mice on a riverboat would have to be very careful not to frighten the passengers.

'Thank you for asking him,' said Lime. And they all nodded—except String, who was already feeling seasick and had his eyes closed.

'The feeling won't last,' Mr Furbank told him kindly. 'Give me a wave as you go past, all of you.'

And they promised they would.

PRAYER STEPS

Praying with a visual aid

You can do this on your own or in a group. Gather some musical or percussion instruments together, or just ordinary objects you can use to make a sound. Think about the way different sounds seem to carry different messages. Can you demonstrate some of these using the instruments and objects? Being pleased? Being angry or impatient? Showing friendship? Having fun? Take time to reflect or discuss how sounds can speak to us.

Praying with the Bible

Use the following passages for personal reflection or discussion.

⭑ **Exodus 4:10–17:** What stopped Moses agreeing to God's plan? How did God try to talk him into it? Is there something we won't agree to for similar reasons?

⭑ **Mark 7:31–37:** What did the people do for the deaf man? What did Jesus do for him? Why didn't Jesus want them to tell anybody?

⭑ **Acts 4:23–31:** What are the signs of the Holy Spirit working in these verses? Are our prayers spoken with one voice? Do we know the courage that comes from God?

⭑ **1 Timothy 2:8:** What does it mean to raise 'innocent hands' (CEV) or 'holy hands' (NIV)? Why is that important? Can we tell if the prayers are to be spoken or silent?

Praying on your own

Do you ever pray out loud when you are on your own? That is how people often used to pray. Try it, as another way you can pray.

Praying in a group

Discuss as a group the things you want to pray about before you start. Write down the subject and some key words on a board. Then if someone doesn't want to pray a long prayer out loud, they can just say the key words for you all to agree on.

Praying it through

Draw your thoughts together in a time of quiet reflection, or use the appropriate version of the prayer below.

Lord, give me the courage and the words to speak for you. Amen

Lord, give us the courage and the words to speak for you. Amen

SPEAKING FOR OURSELVES: LEARNING PRAYERS OR PRAYING OUR OWN WORDS

Let my words and my thoughts be pleasing to you, Lord.
PSALM 19:14

INTRODUCTION

Should we pray in our own words, or use words that have been written down and prayed many times before? Using the same words that have been said for hundreds of years can be very powerful, and bring us closer to all those people who have prayed in the same way. We can enjoy using someone else's carefully chosen words, just as we sing the words of a well-known song or hymn. At the same time, using our own words can help us to be more open with God and to mean what we say. We can talk to God as we would to a friend; we can just be ourselves.

We find examples of both in the Bible. In Luke's Gospel, Simeon prayed as he held the baby Jesus in the temple. He used some of his own words and some words from scripture. In the book of Acts, Ananias talked to God about Paul, just as if they were having an ordinary conversation. In Revelation, there is a picture of heaven where people are singing a song by Moses, written hundreds of years before.

THE BEST PANCAKE

The Annual Kettlemarsh Village Pancake Competition was ready to be judged. There were ten entries in the under-twelves section. The pancakes had to be perfectly made, and filled with a very special filling. Contestants were allowed to use any recipe they liked for the filling. There were two judges—the lady Mayor, who enjoyed tasting things, and Mr Dawes, the head teacher, who worried what the children had put into their cooking.

'Tell me about your pancake,' the Mayor asked Meredith. 'What filling have you used?'

'Squashed bananas, peanut butter and ice cream,' Meredith told her proudly. Mr Dawes shuddered.

The judges walked on, looking carefully at how well the pancakes had been cooked, checking there were no burnt bits scraped off.

Sam felt nervous as the Mayor approached her. 'And what about the filling in your pancake?'

'It's a special recipe,' said Sam. 'My mum taught it to me. Her grandmother gave it to her.'

'And what does it have in it?' asked Mr Dawes.

Sam ticked off the ingredients on her fingers, 'Fresh pineapple, grated lemon peel, caramel sauce, whipped cream and something secret.'

Mr Dawes wondered what the secret ingredient could be, and whether it was yucky.

'Did you make the caramel sauce yourself?' asked the Mayor.

'Yes,' said Sam, remembering the smell when she'd burnt the saucepan.

They moved on down the line, to Sam's friend Joseph. Joseph wasn't sure what had gone into his filling. He'd found a recipe for apple and decided to start with that. Then he found the apples weren't ripe and had cut up an orange instead. He'd meant to put in some sultanas but they'd turned out to be lentils, and he'd had to fish them all out again. Then the sugar had run out, so he'd used honey. The recipe had mentioned a touch of cinnamon, but he'd used ginger because he thought it smelled more exciting. Then he'd added something else he'd found in the fridge. His mum told him later it was grated carrot. Finally, he'd stirred in some melted chocolate.

'Is it a very old recipe?' asked the Mayor.

'Not really,' said Joseph—which was true, at least by the time he'd finished with it.

Then the tasting began. 'Too much fat in the pan,' said the Mayor, moving down the line. 'You've fried them. Nice texture, but the filling is too bland.'

Then she came to Sam's pancake, and helped herself to a small slice. She smiled. 'This is superb! And the filling is wonderful. What a great recipe to have in your family.'

Sam felt very pleased. Then the judges got to Joseph.

'It's very good. Unusual. Interesting mixture of flavours. What do you think, Mr Dawes?'

'Interesting,' said Mr Dawes, who was surprised to find he liked it. 'Brave.'

'Yes, brave.'

Sam and Joseph held their breath. They were sure the judges liked theirs best. But which of them was going to win?

Mr Dawes and the Mayor talked with each other quietly for a moment. And then the Mayor announced: 'We declare these two the joint winners! Both pancakes are delicious, but for different reasons.'

Then all the contestants were allowed to taste all the pancakes.

'I still like mine best,' thought Sam.

'I still like mine best,' thought Joseph. 'I wonder what it was?'

PRAYER STEPS

Praying with a visual aid

Have open a road map or OS map. In a group or on your own, consider the different routes you can take to travel between two major cities. Reflect on or discuss which route you might prefer. Would you choose the fastest roads? Or do you prefer the small minor roads and why? Is there somewhere else you might want to visit as you travel? Are you someone who uses maps, or do you just like to find your own way there?

Praying with the Bible

Use the following passages for personal reflection or discussion.

✱ **Psalm 19:** People sometimes pray verse 14 before preaching. What is the prayer asking? How does this last verse arise from the whole psalm?

* **Luke 2:25–32:** How does this story connect with the past and with the future? How does Simeon speak about Jesus? What do we know of Simeon's own relationship with God?
* **Acts 9:10–19:** What strikes you about Ananias and his conversation with God? Do we expect to talk so openly with God?
* **Revelation 15:2–4:** Traditionally sung in the synagogue, these verses express the greatness of God. Who is the Lamb, and why is this his song? How can we remind ourselves of God's greatness as we worship him?

Praying on your own

Think about the prayer written below. In what ways might God bring light into darkness? Pray the words as they are written, or pray in your own words that God would bring light into our world.

Praying in a group

As a group, write a prayer together. Make it special to your group. Pray for each other; pray for a good time together; pray for those who are in need. Thank God for all his goodness and kindness. You may like to use the prayer you've written or the prayer below from time to time when your group comes together.

Praying it through

Draw your thoughts together in a time of quiet reflection, or use the prayer below, which was written hundreds of years ago, asking God to protect us as night falls or we face any kind of danger. People still use these words today.

Lighten our darkness, Lord, we pray and in your great mercy defend us from all perils and dangers of this night, for the love of your only Son, our Saviour Jesus Christ. Amen

ALL KINDS OF PRAYERS: USING THE GIFTS OF GOD

> **The Spirit has given each of us a special way of serving others.**
> 1 CORINTHIANS 12:7

INTRODUCTION

God has sent us the Holy Spirit to teach us and guide us to know him better.

The Spirit gives special gifts to us. For instance, he gives us the gift of using words so that we can tell others about Jesus or so that we can pray and worship. We all have different gifts, but they are given so that we can serve God's people and not just please ourselves.

In the Old Testament, when Moses was struggling as leader of the Israelites, God gave his Spirit to a group of people so that they could help Moses lead. In John's Gospel, Jesus said that God's Spirit would go on teaching the church all that we need to know. In his letter to the church in Corinth, Paul tells us that there are all sorts of gifts God gives to help us serve him, but they all come from God's Spirit.

 ## THE SCHOOL BUS

'This school bus is hopeless,' said Asha. 'It's always going off course. Last week a whole class ended up in the wrong galaxy.'

The four children stepped out on to the strange planet. Its surface was crunchy and soft, like walking on cornflakes.

'What do we do now?' asked Greg.

'We wait,' said Jason. 'Someone's bound to come looking for us.'

Martine frowned back at the spacecraft. 'I think the software's out of date.'

Jason pressed the buttons on his mobile phone. 'I'd better phone the school. Hello? Mr Lee? We've got a bit of a problem…'. He talked for a while and then turned to the others. 'Mr Lee says he'll contact the bus company and get them to send another vehicle. He says while we wait, we can do some interesting research for our geography essay.'

Martine groaned and climbed back up the steps. 'I'm going to try to fix that computer,' she said. 'I can't stand geography.'

Greg had already started scraping up some of the cornflakes to put in his school bag. Then he spotted a small green bush some distance away and decided to pick some leaves for his collection. He yanked at a handful, but the mound gave a shriek and ran away. Greg chased it for a while and then stopped to pick up more objects.

Jason's mobile rang. 'Yes? Mr Lee? All right, I'll tell them.'

'What was that about?' asked Asha, watching Jason's face.

'Mr Lee says we may be here a long time. The bus company is very sorry, but there's no bus available till the morning.'

'That's OK!' said Greg. 'I've got loads to look at. There's a whole lake over there. I want to get some of it in a jar.'

'You're weird, Greg,' said Asha. 'You'd be happy anywhere.' She took some photos with her mobile and started to draw the landscape in her sketchbook. Her eye kept going to a fascinating group of tall plants, twisting round on their stems like corkscrews, their petals long and feathery. The shadow from each plant fell across the ground, casting a speckled pattern. Asha turned the page and began a new sketch.

As she worked with her coloured pencils, Asha noticed that the pattern on the ground was changing. She kept drawing, slightly puzzled. And then it made sense. Each plant was casting two shadows. She looked up at the sky behind her head.

'Look,' she called to the others. 'This planet has got two suns. One's brighter than the other.'

'Well spotted,' said Jason. 'We can work out where we are now.'

Some time later, Jason found he was shivering. 'It's getting dark, everyone,' he said. 'We need to search the bus for food.'

They climbed back inside the spacecraft. Asha discovered several packets of rather hard biscuits in a locker and shared them around. Martine came out from the flight deck. 'Uh, I think it's OK now. I'm just reinstalling the navigation program from the backup. I've quarantined a couple of dodgy bits, and then I'll get online to the bus company for them to give it a test run.'

'What is she saying?' asked Greg.

'Never mind,' said Asha. 'She's a genius. She can make it work.'

Within 20 minutes they were back in space, travelling home. Greg showed them all he'd collected: cornflakes; a tiny red shell; soft, spongy blue plants; and a tadpole creature in a jar. A beep sounded, and Mr Lee came on-screen. 'Well done, all of you,' he said, as he heard their report. 'Jason, I knew you'd be sensible and look after everyone. Greg, you always make the best of every situation. You make us all feel better. Martine, you have the skill to go straight to the heart of the problem and sort it out. And Asha, you have an eye for what the rest of us would miss. Well done. You make a good team.' The screen went blank. Greg looked at his collection. 'Maybe we've got time to stop off at another planet on the way home,' he suggested.

'Maybe not,' said Jason.

PRAYER STEPS

Praying with a visual aid

In a group or on your own, look through the contents of a tool box, or a drawer of kitchen implements. In a time of quiet reflection or discussion, think about each of the items. What are they used for? Can they be used for other things as well? Can they be used on their own? What might damage them? Would one item on its own be enough?

Praying with the Bible

Use the following passages for personal reflection or discussion.

★ **Numbers 11:24–30:** Moses could not lead alone. What was his response to the gift of God being shared out? What was Joshua's response? Are we happy to see others given the same gifts as us?

* **Joel 2:28–32**: These words were quoted at Pentecost by Peter. What is the significance of the Spirit being given to everyone? Where are all these signs pointing?
* **John 16:12–15**: What is the role of the Spirit in these verses? How do we see the Spirit accomplishing this in our church?
* **1 Corinthians 12:1–11**: What principles does Paul emphasize? What is the basis for unity? Who decides which gifts people are given?

Praying on your own

Do you know what spiritual gifts God has given you? Ask God to show you if you are not sure and ask him to help you use them in the best way.

Praying in a group

What are the spiritual gifts you think God has given to people in your group? Are any of you good at praying? Are any of you good at speaking about Jesus? Do any of you have strong faith? Do any of you encourage others? Talk about it together and see if you agree.

Praying it through

Draw your thoughts together in a time of quiet reflection, or use the appropriate version of the prayer below.

Dear Lord, thank you for the gifts you have given me. Help me to use them so that others can know you better. Amen

Dear Lord, thank you for the gifts you have given us. Help us to use them so that others can know you better. Amen

WHEN WE ARE WEAK: HOW GOD HELPS US TO PRAY

The Spirit is here to help us.
ROMANS 8:26

INTRODUCTION

Praying isn't always easy. There are times when we feel weak or upset, and we find it very difficult to know how to pray. God will help us even though we are struggling to speak to him.

In the Old Testament, once when Daniel was praying, God sent an angel to strengthen and encourage him. In the Gospels, the father of a sick boy said he believed in Jesus but asked Jesus to help him believe more. In his letter to the church in Rome, Paul tells us that the Holy Spirit understands what we need to pray and prays for us.

S.O.S.

'Distress call coming in!' The radio operator swivelled round in his chair. 'A dinghy drifting off Parry's Rock. Two young boys in the water, clinging to the side.'

Within seconds the men were running the lifeboat down into the sea. Soon the motor was churning up the water, the boat bouncing through the waves. Two very wet, cold and frightened boys were pulled on board. The dinghy was fastened and towed behind.

'I didn't know what to do!' The older boy's teeth were chattering with cold. 'Davy fell in and I tried to pull him back on board. Then the boat sort of swung over and I fell in, too. I shouted and shouted, but no one could hear me.'

'Someone radioed in and told us about you,' said one of the men. 'Good job, too. Your brother looks all in.'

Jerry looked at his young brother, wrapped in a special blanket but still pale and motionless.

'He'll be all right,' said the man kindly, sensing the boy's anxiety. 'What were you doing out there on your own?'

'My dad taught us to sail. He's a fisherman. The sea was calm. The sky was clear. It was Davy. He slipped. And then I…'. Jerry felt ashamed of himself. His dad had told him so often how to help someone back on board, but, seeing his young brother in the water, he'd panicked.

'Well, you've learnt something,' said the man. 'I don't expect you'll ever forget it.'

'And I never did,' said Jerry. He looked round at the faces of the schoolchildren gathered in the boat station. 'That's why I joined the lifeboats, over 30 years ago. Of course, the boats have changed since then. There's better equipment, better surveillance. But I never forgot the person who radioed in and saved us both.'

'Who was it?' called out a girl from the back row.

'That's what I wanted to know. I didn't find out for a few days. Then my dad went to the lifeboat station and asked them. It turns out there was a man flying a light aircraft over the sea, just out for an afternoon from the aerodrome. He used to be a pilot during the war. He saw my brother and me in the water, and he knew we needed help. I met him afterwards. I was able to thank him.'

Jerry looked out over the grey waves curling on to the sand. 'I owe my life to that pilot. He sent a message straight to the lifeboat station, while I could only shout for help to an empty sea. Now gather round, and I'll show you what we stow on board the lifeboat. It might help us rescue someone, like someone rescued me.'

PRAYER STEPS

Praying with a visual aid

Find a dial radio. On your own or in a group, dial the radio just out of tune, so that you can hear the noise but the words are muffled. Listen for a while and then adjust the tuning so that you can hear clearly. Do you feel your communications are muffled sometimes, and you are not getting through to people? Does this make you feel angry, despondent or frightened? Do you ever feel that other people seem out of tune? Does God seem muffled? How do you think we sound to him? Take time for personal reflection or discussion.

Praying with the Bible

Use the following passages for personal reflection or discussion.

★ **Daniel 10:2–19:** How does Daniel respond to the visions he is given? What are the different ways the angel brings encouragement to him?

✳ **Mark 9:14–29**: How did the disciples show they were weak? How did the father of the boy respond to his own weakness? How do we respond to Jesus in our weakness?

✳ **Romans 8:23–27**: What are we waiting for in the future? What should our attitude be meanwhile? How does the Spirit help us?

✳ **1 Corinthians 2:10–12**: What is the role of the Spirit in these verses? What insight does this give us?

Praying on your own

Think of someone who knows you really well, perhaps a friend or family member. Do you ever feel they know what you are thinking? Think about the fact that God knows you even better than they do.

Praying in a group

One of you mimes an activity, while the others have to guess what it is. It could be cleaning your teeth or driving a car or climbing a mountain. The one who guesses right has the next go. In the same way, God can tell what you are trying to pray, even though you may be struggling to use words.

Praying it through

Draw your thoughts together in a time of quiet reflection, or use the appropriate version of the prayer below.

Dear Lord, you know what I want to say, and what I find hard to put into words. Thank you that you hear the prayers I don't know how to pray. Amen

Dear Lord, you know what we want to say, and what we find hard to put into words. Thank you that you hear the prayers we don't know how to pray. Amen

THE SWORD OF THE SPIRIT: GOD SPEAKS TO US THROUGH THE BIBLE

> Please, Lord, hear my prayer and give me the understanding that comes from your word.
>
> PSALM 119:169

INTRODUCTION

Sometimes God answers our prayers by speaking to us through the Bible. We can find guidance or advice, or read about what happened to someone in the same situation. It's helpful if reading the Bible becomes part of our regular prayer life. Verses from the Bible can also be included in our prayers, to help us to pray.

The writer of Psalm 119 prayed for God's teachings in scripture to fill his life. In Luke's Gospel, we see that Jesus, even as a young boy, knew so much scripture that he could debate with the wise teachers in the temple. In his first letter, Peter tells us that the prophets who wrote the scriptures did so for our sake, so that we might know about Jesus.

 ## THE CASTLE MAZE

Amy read the notice nailed across the swing gate and frowned. '"Closed. Keep Out." Oh, boring!'

Her brother Danny leant against the gate and it creaked open. 'Come on. Dad will be ages looking round the castle. You know he'll want to know the history of everything.'

Inside, the castle maze was overgrown and neglected, the pathways covered in dead leaves, and statues everywhere: animals, figures, vases—many of them chipped and broken. Danny's friend, Anil, touched the carved head of a stone badger. 'We're the only ones here. It's a bit weird.'

'Which way do we go?' asked Amy. She noticed a book lying on a marble table along one of the paths and went over to have a look. 'Hey, look at this!' she called. 'It says, "To help you through the maze."'

Danny picked up the book and opened it. The pages were filled with small, scratchy handwriting. 'It's magic,' he said. 'A book of spells. Let's take it with us.' They carried on past the table and followed the path round the corner. A pile of rotting wooden sticks blocked their way.

'We'll have to use magic.' Danny held the book up in his hands and said loudly to the sticks, 'Vanish!' Nothing happened. 'It's not working,' he complained. He started kicking the sticks angrily.

'Give it to me.' Anil took the book and glanced through it. 'It's not magic,' he said. 'It's just meant to be helpful. It says here, "Be wise. Don't be stupid."'

Amy shrugged. 'Well, we are being stupid. We need to turn round and go back past the table.'

They retraced their steps and took the other path. As they walked on, the hedges seemed to get thicker and more over-grown. Soon the light above their heads was almost blotted out.

'Are you sure this is the right way?' asked Amy. 'It's very dark. I can hardly see.'

Anil opened the book and was just able to read a sentence. 'It says here, "Keep going."'

'Keep going where?' asked Danny.

'Just "Keep going." And "Don't be scared." Why should we be scared?'

They scrambled on, pushing through the tangled hedges, taking one turning after another.

'We must be nearly in the middle by now.' Danny stopped suddenly. 'What's that noise?'

They all heard it—the sound of strange breathing, like a huge animal. They could see ahead of them where the tunnel opened out into a small, square terrace. As they approached it, the breathing got louder.

'There!' cried Danny. 'It's in there!' He was pointing to the far side of the terrace where the path continued. Out of the darkness, two yellow eyes gazed at them hungrily.

'It's only a statue,' said Anil. But at that moment the eyes moved to look at him.

'It's alive!' cried Amy. 'What is it?'

'I don't know,' said Anil. 'What shall I do?'

'Hit it with the book.'

Anil held the book high, ready to throw it, but the creature stayed where it was. And then they turned and ran, stumbling over their own feet, taking one path after another, getting as far away as possible.

'We're lost,' gasped Danny, slowing. 'What does the book say about being lost?'

Slumping down for a rest, Amy began to flick through the pages. 'Hey. It's got stories in it.' She read for a while. 'There's a story here about some people lost in a maze for days and days. In the end, they get rescued.'

'I wish someone would rescue us,' Danny grumbled.

'We could shout for help,' said Anil.

'No, thanks. That thing might hear us.'

'So, we do what the book says.' Anil struggled to his feet. 'We keep going.'

Wearily, they started walking. They were so tired; at first they didn't notice the young boy who was walking beside them.

'Oh! You made me jump!' cried Amy. 'How long have you been there?'

The boy was about their own age. He was barefoot, and bits of twig clung to his clothes. 'I saw you come in. There's a gate in the hedge just round the corner. I waited for you.' The boy led them along a pathway overgrown with weeds and nettles and pushed open a creaking wooden gate. The children fell out on to the grass, and lay there, recovering.

'Do you live here?' asked Amy when they had their breath back.

'I used to. My dad was the gardener. He planted the maze years ago, but the new owners have let it go wild. There're some strange things in there.'

'We know.' Danny thought of the yellow eyes.

'I see you found my book.' The boy took it back from Anil.

'It's a weird guidebook,' said Anil.

The boy smiled cheerfully. 'Most guidebooks are for people who know where they are. This is for people who are lost.'

The children crossed the lawn back to the castle. They arrived just as a tall figure came out through a side door, clutching a thick catalogue.

'Wonderful place. Extraordinary,' said their dad. 'Huge. I'm surprised I found my way out. What have you lot been doing?'

Danny pulled a face. 'You'd be a-maze-d,' he said.

PRAYER STEPS

Praying with a visual aid

On your own or in a group, take a piece of card, some sticky tape and some coloured pens and make a lighthouse. You might like to put a hand torch or bulb inside so that the lighthouse is illuminated. Reflect on or discuss the purpose of a lighthouse. Consider how it represents both safety and danger. How does it act as a warning? How does it act as a guide? What is the role of the lighthouse keeper, and what action needs to be taken by those aboard ship?

Praying with the Bible

Use the following passages for personal reflection or discussion.

* **Psalm 119:169–176:** Is it enough to think of God's teaching as rules? What is the relationship between God and the writer? What is the writer's prayer?
* **Luke 2:41–52:** What amazed the teachers in the temple? How did Jesus know so much? What did the scriptures mean to him?
* **Ephesians 5:14–20:** How should scripture become part of our lives? How should we live in the light of Christ? What type of prayer is talked about here?

★ **1 Peter 1:10–12:** What is the role of the Spirit in these verses? What did the prophets understand about Jesus? Where do we read their words?

Praying on your own

Read aloud Psalm 119:169–176. Read it several times and see which verse in it becomes the prayer you want to pray.

Praying in a group

Create a maze on the floor using masking tape. You will need to have paths that divide in two so there are choices. Then form two teams. Each team needs to make some 'Bible clues' to help you round. For example, put a drawing of a lion on the right path and a spider on the wrong path. Then give a Bible reference for Daniel in the lion's den. Or you could have a picture of a lamp on the right path and a mouse on the wrong path and the Bible reference Psalm 119:105. Then each team in turn tries to go round the maze using the other team's clues.

Praying it through

Draw your thoughts together in a time of quiet reflection, or use the appropriate version of the prayer below.

Lord, thank you that your word is a lamp that gives light wherever I walk. Amen (from Psalm 119:105).

Lord, thank you that your word is a lamp that gives light wherever we walk. Amen (from Psalm 119:105).

I DON'T BELIEVE IT!: HOW MUCH FAITH DO WE NEED TO PRAY?

> 'Everything you ask for in prayer will be yours, if you only have faith.'
>
> MARK 11:24

INTRODUCTION

How much faith do we need before God answers our prayers? Is it our fault if our prayers aren't answered? And what if we really believe something, and it still doesn't happen? Faith is not just making ourselves believe that God will do something we ask. Faith is our whole relationship with God—whether we trust him, whether we are willing to follow him, whether we want to see him working in our lives. Faith means trusting and believing God, even when something has happened that seems to make no sense or is hard to bear.

In the Old Testament, Abraham trusted God when God promised him many, many descendants. God was pleased that Abraham believed him. In Mark's Gospel, Jesus told his disciples that if they had faith in God, their prayers would be answered. Prayer and faith go together. In John's Gospel, Jesus asked his disciples if they would continue to follow him. Peter replied that Jesus spoke words that gave life, and that they did have faith in him.

THE FLYING SHIP

Two men grabbed Johann and pulled him towards the edge of the cliff. 'So men can fly, can they?' cried one. Johann bent his body backwards, trying to resist the efforts of the men. Below him, the sea rolled on to the rocks, white spray hanging in the air like a cloud. 'Let's see you fly.'

An arm swung back to push Johann forward over the edge, but suddenly the flat blade of a sword landed on the man's shoulder.

'Let him go!' commanded a voice. 'Stand back, all of you.'

The group retreated a few steps, staring at the newcomer. He was tall, dressed in tattered clothes and wore a breastplate and helmet as well as a sword. 'Now,' he demanded. 'What has this lad done?'

'His master is dead,' answered a woman. 'In his house we found strange papers, written in his master's hand. We burnt them. His master taught him that men could fly like birds if they had a mind to it. We're just seeing if he was right.' A laugh went around the group.

'Is this sorcery?' the stranger asked Johann. Johann shook his head, too sick with fear to speak.

'I will question him alone,' the man declared. 'I have travelled to far places, but I have never seen a man fly. Stand back, all of you, and leave him with me.'

Grumbling, but reluctant to challenge an armed man, the villagers wandered away.

'My name is Roy de Marche,' said the stranger, introducing

himself. 'I own some land here and I'm returning to build myself a home. Who was your master?'

Johann brightened. 'He was my teacher. He knew everything. And he had ideas. He believed that one day people would be able to fly. Not alone but in a vessel built for that purpose.'

Roy shook his head. 'Impossible. If you drop a stone or even a leaf, it will fall to the ground; it can't fly.'

Johann pointed across the sea to where a line of ships were sailing. 'If you drop a stone into a pond, it will sink. And yet great ships now sail on the sea. Why shouldn't there be ships that sail through the air? All you have to do is set the sails for the wind to carry you along.'

'Did your master make such a ship?' Roy asked him.

Johann hesitated, as if unsure whether to trust the man. 'He drew plans. The villagers burnt them. But he also made a small ship out of wood and cloth. I will show you if you like. I've hidden it in the woods.'

Johann led Roy along the cliff path towards the edge of the wood. He had forgotten his fear. Reaching into the hollow of a tree, he took out an object wrapped in cloth. Inside was a wooden hull, with three sails set either side attached to a rigid frame. A small wooden peg acted as a rudder at the back, and the front was shaped like the bow of a ship.

'It is a strange sight,' said Roy. 'You tell me it can fly?'

'Don't you believe it?' asked Johann.

'I believe nothing. My comrades lie dead on the field of battle, and my heart is heavy. If this marvel could fly, it might teach me there is some purpose in believing.'

Johann adjusted the rudder and sails, held up his arms and sent the craft skimming between the trees. The wind flowed between its sails, lifting it and keeping it steady. Gradually the craft slowed and floated down to land gently on the grass.

'Was that flying?' asked Roy.

'It's a start,' said Johann. 'It needs some device to keep pushing it through the air. Throwing it does not send it far enough. Perhaps a small explosion would do or many small explosions, using gunpowder.'

Roy laughed. 'I believe you will do it,' he said. 'Your master was right. I am sure men will fly like birds. I can see you will never give up. Let me build a place for you on my land where you can continue your work. But I warn you, no explosions near my house.'

Johann was wrapping the cloth back around the craft. He hardly heard Roy speaking, but he followed him through the woods, his mind working out what to do next.

PRAYER STEPS

Praying with a visual aid

On your own or in a group take some Post-it notes and look around you, wherever you are right now. What are you trusting at the moment? It could be the chair you are sitting on or the ceiling above you or many other things. Put a Post-it note on each item. In what way do you trust these things? Do you trust the people who've made them? How might trust be damaged? Take time to reflect or discuss how faith and trust go together.

Praying with the Bible

Use the following passages for personal reflection or discussion.

* **Jeremiah 32:1–15:** Why did God ask Jeremiah to buy the field? What situation was Jeremiah in at the time? How is this a picture of faith?
* **Mark 11:20–26:** What lesson did Jesus want the disciples to learn about prayer? How did he want his words about moving mountains to be understood? What is the connection between forgiveness and having faith?
* **John 6:66–69:** Why did Jesus ask his disciples such a question? What do we learn about faith from Peter's answer? Can we make the same response?
* **Romans 4:18–25:** What themes of death and life do we find in these verses? What is the connection with faith?

Praying on your own

Is there someone whose words you always believe because you know you can trust them? It could be a friend or someone in your family or just someone you know. How do you know you can believe them? We may not always understand what Jesus says in the Bible, but do we trust and believe him? Read John 6:66–69 to see Peter's answer.

Praying in a group

Play the game 'Call my bluff', where you have to guess who is telling the truth and who is making up the answers. We may not always understand what Jesus says in the Bible, but do we trust and believe him? Read John 6:66–69 to see Peter's answer.

Praying it through

Draw your thoughts together in a time of quiet reflection, or use the appropriate version of the prayer below.

Lord Jesus, help me to believe in you and trust you. Help my faith to grow. Amen

Lord Jesus, help us to believe in you and trust you. Help our faith to grow. Amen

REMEMBER WHEN...:
LOOKING BACK AT
ANSWERED PRAYER

> **Remember his miracles and all his wonders.**
> 1 CHRONICLES 16:12a

INTRODUCTION

Remembering all that God has done for us in the past encourages us to pray. It reminds us how good he is, and it also helps us believe that he will answer our prayers.

In the Old Testament, the Israelites were taught to remember all that God had done by telling stories to each other, by learning scripture, by having special festivals, by eating special food. In the Gospels, Jesus asks his disciples to remember him as they eat bread and drink wine. Christians today still remember all that Jesus has done through the service of Holy Communion.

 ## GRANDMA'S TIN BOX

'There'll be loads of spiders!' said Ellie, poking the end of a tennis racket into the dark corner.

Miles pulled aside the basket of toys, and something scurried away up the wall.

'Massive!' he said. 'I bet there are mice as well.'

The two of them dragged the basket into the centre of the garage floor. 'Hey, look at this!' cried Miles. 'It's my old ambulance. The light flashes when the wheels go round. It doesn't work any more.'

'That's because it hasn't got any wheels.' Ellie put her hand in the basket and took out a cardboard box. 'My farm set. Oh, I hope it's all here.' She began laying out fences, animals, trees and a duck pond on the floor.

'Come on,' said Miles. 'We're meant to be sorting it out, not playing. Oh, I remember this.'

'My doll!' Ellie snatched it from him. 'Bibby. You were horrid to her. You buried her once.'

'You agreed.'

'I was only two. You told me she'd come back to life. Mum had to bribe you to say where you'd put her.'

Miles turned back to the basket. 'Well, she's all mouldy now. I should dump her. Hey, I don't remember this.'

Ellie peered over his arm. 'It's a tin box. Whose is it? It looks really old.'

The pattern on the box was of tiny roses, pushed out so that the surface felt bumpy. A green ribbon printed around the sides made it look like a present. The lid was hinged, with one of the hinges bent at an angle. Miles pressed his fingers against the lid and pulled it open. Inside, a piece of thin white cloth was carefully wrapped round some objects.

'Give it to me!' ordered Ellie.

Her brother swung away from her and pulled at the cloth. Tiny china figures peeked out. Miles placed the box on the floor, and one by one they picked up the figures and examined them. One was an elephant, sleek and grey, with shiny white tusks. Another was a young boy dressed as a shepherd, a sheepdog curled around his feet. Among the rest were a ballerina, some soldiers in redcoats, a pair of tiny kittens and a prancing horse.

'Where did they come from?' asked Ellie in wonder.

'They're mine,' said Mum, when they showed her the box. 'Oh dear, I'd forgotten they were there. They're mine. At least, they were your grandmother's. They were the only toys she had.'

She opened the lid and rummaged through with one finger. 'She gave them to me because she wanted me to remember my grandad. When she was a little girl, he was away from home a lot. Every time he came back, he'd bring a new china toy with him. When she missed him, she'd open the box and remember all the times he'd come home and what fun they'd had. Then she'd add the new toy to her tin. They must have got into the garage when we moved here. I should really keep them somewhere special.'

'Can I have them?' asked Ellie.

'One day, yes. Maybe you can share them between you.'

'What was your grandad like?' asked Miles.

Mum smiled. 'He was a big man. Always in a suit, but not too smart. And he laughed a lot. I was very small, so I remember him as a giant. A jolly giant.' She took the tin and placed it on a shelf in the kitchen. 'It can live there for the moment. Now, what about your toys? How are you getting on?' And she followed them out to the garage, to see what they'd chosen to keep.

PRAYER STEPS

Praying with a visual aid

On your own or in a group, write a sentence where each word begins with the first letter of one of the colours of the rainbow—Red, Orange, Yellow, Green, Blue, Indigo, Violet. The sentence needs to be easy, to help you remember it. Think of the different ways we remember special moments or people in our lives, such as photographs, letters, jewellery. Take a moment to reflect on or discuss the importance of remembering.

Praying with the Bible

Use the following passages for personal reflection or discussion.

* ✯ **Exodus 13:3–10:** What are the Israelites being asked to remember? How are they to remember? How will remembering affect them and their families?
* ✯ **1 Chronicles 16:7–36:** How do praise, worship and remembering work together in this song? How will this influence other nations? Are we aware of similarities to our worship?
* ✯ **Luke 22:19:** How are we to remember Jesus, and what are we to remember? How central are acts of remembrance to our lives?
* ✯ **2 Peter 1:3–15:** What does Peter want God's people to remember? Why is it especially important they do so?

Praying on your own

Think of one thing that has happened to you where you are certain God has been good to you. Think about it for a while. What does it teach you about God?

Praying in a group

Some of you may have stories about the way God has answered prayer. Take time to listen to them. Write a list on a board of things God has done for you or given to you. Then say a prayer to thank God for his goodness.

Praying it through

Draw your thoughts together in a time of quiet reflection, or use the appropriate version of the prayer below.

Heavenly Father, I thank you as I remember Jesus. I remember his love for me, that he came to earth to live among us and that he died for me and rose again. I also thank you for... (your own prayer). Amen

Heavenly Father, we thank you as we remember Jesus. We remember his love for us, that he came to earth to live among us and that he died for us and rose again. We also thank you for... (your own prayer). Amen

TEACH US TO PRAY: LEARNING HOW JESUS PRAYED

> **'Lord, teach us to pray.'**
> LUKE 11:1a

INTRODUCTION

Jesus taught his disciples how to pray, using words that have come to be known as the Lord's Prayer. We can also learn a lot about prayer from the way Jesus prayed:

* He prayed with confidence, knowing his Father in heaven was listening.
* He prayed alone, early in the morning, in quiet places such as hilltops.
* He joined in public prayer and worship in the synagogues.
* He gave thanks and praised God for many things.
* He prayed when he was facing death on the cross.
* In his prayers he said that he would do all that his Father in heaven wanted.
* He prayed in faith, trusting that his Father would raise him from the dead.

 ## DEAR REUBEN

Dear Reuben,

I'm sending you this letter to let you know I'm all right. Someone here is a scribe, and he's writing it for me. Tell Mum and Dad I'm fine. I've been in Galilee now for three weeks. So much is happening, it's awesome. I've watched people who couldn't walk start dancing, and even someone blind was made to see! I listen to all that Jesus says, and I really believe he's going to set Israel free.

Something happened this morning. It made me think about him in a different way. A whole crowd of us slept all night on the grassy hillside by the lake as it was too far to the town and the night air was warm enough. I wrapped my cloak round me and put my head on a stone. I woke very early in the morning. The sky over the lake was the faintest pink, and there were loads of birds still huddled along the shoreline. A breeze was blowing; it made a whistling sound through the ropes and nets on the sand. I could see some fishermen out on the water, just grey shapes moving. They were getting ready to come ashore, pulling in their nets and taking down the sails. Then I saw him—Jesus. He was walking away from the sleeping bodies, away up the hillside. I rolled to my feet and began following him. He stepped quietly between the rocks, striding on without turning back. He looked as if he knew exactly where he was going.

We came to a part of the hilltop overlooking the lake, far away from everything. He stretched first of all, his arms reached up high, and he took a deep breath. It made me want to do the same. My body felt all crumpled after being asleep and my muscles longed to stretch. But I didn't think he knew I was there, so I kept very still. And then he began to pray, talking to God. He called him 'Father', just like I do with Dad. I haven't heard anyone talk to God like that before.

He prayed lots of things I didn't understand. I couldn't make out if he was happy or sad. There seemed to be something terrible he was going to have to face. And yet he also said that he was ready to do it. I suppose he meant he was going to start a war against the Romans. I'm ready to fight by his side if he does. Don't worry, I know God is with us in this.

There was something else he said. He quoted a psalm. He quoted lots of psalms, I remember, but this one really stayed in my head. He said: 'Father, here I am. As scripture says about me, I have come to do what you want.' He said it with such love in his voice, as if he loved God more than anything. And I could tell he really meant it. It made me feel the same, as if I longed more than anything to do what God wanted. Don't laugh. It really felt like that, the most important thing I'd ever heard. And exciting. Very exciting. I don't know what's going to happen, but I do know that God has something in mind.

Then, when the sky was all broken up with orange and purple lines and the ground was beginning to warm up, he turned to go back. I was crouched behind a rock, and he walked straight past me on his way down. He'd only gone a few steps further when I heard him say quietly, without looking round, 'Come on, son.' We didn't talk. I felt as if part of him was still in another place, in a special place, so I hung back and walked behind him. Just as we reached the grassy bank above the lake, some men ran forward towards him. 'Master, master, we've been looking for you,' they cried. 'There's a whole crowd of people waiting to see you. They're ready to listen. Come on, there are hundreds of them!'

I wondered if he would mind—the noise and the crowd and the demands on him. But then I realized he didn't mind. It's why he was there. And the same love he felt for God seemed to be reaching out to them as well. I tried to feel the same, but it was hard. I wanted to be back on the hilltop, just with him, knowing that God was there. But I'd made a choice, so I went with him to see what would happen.

The scribe says he won't write any more unless I pay him twice as much, so I'll end here. Peace be with you,

Your brother, Eban

PRAYER STEPS

Praying with a visual aid

On your own or in a group, draw round your feet on several different pieces of paper and lay the footprints across the room. Imagine someone stepping in your footprints and following you. Reflect or discuss what it feels like to have someone copy you. Does it make you more careful what you say and do? Who are the people you have copied? What have you learnt from them? Is this a good way to learn?

Praying with the Bible

Use the following passages for personal reflection or discussion.

* **Matthew 26:36–46:** What is the purpose of prayer in this account? What did Jesus want from his disciples?
* **Mark 1:35–38:** How do you think the private prayer of Jesus connected with his public ministry? Are we eager to be alone to pray?
* **Luke 11:1–4:** How did Jesus teach his disciples to pray? What can we learn about prayer from these words?
* **Hebrews 10:5–10:** What does Jesus show us about God's will? What does he show us about himself? Are we prepared to say we are here to do God's will?

Praying on your own

Read the words of the Lord's Prayer written overleaf. Think about the words 'your will be done, on earth as in heaven'. What do you think that means?

Praying in a group

Write your own letter, either in pairs or on your own, describing what it would have been like to be one of the disciples with Jesus. Take some moments of quiet to imagine yourself there.

Praying it through

Draw your thoughts together in a time of quiet reflection, or use the prayer overleaf.

Our Father in heaven,
hallowed be your name,
your kingdom come,
your will be done,
on earth as in heaven.
Give us today our daily bread.
Forgive us our sins
as we forgive those who sin against us.
Lead us not into temptation
but deliver us from evil.
For the kingdom, the power,
and the glory are yours
now and for ever.
Amen

BEFORE DAWN:
REGULAR TIMES OF PRAYER

> **Daniel... knelt down in prayer three times a day.**
> DANIEL 6:10

INTRODUCTION

We can pray to God anytime and anywhere, but many people have regular times of prayer every day. They also meet with others to pray at church every Sunday. It is easy to pray only when we feel like it, but then we can forget about God unless we need something. Having a regular time of prayer builds our relationship with God. It also strengthens us and prepares us for the day.

People all through the Bible prayed at regular times. In the Old Testament, Daniel prayed three times a day. In the Gospels, Jesus went to the synagogue regularly every Sabbath. In the book of Acts, Peter and John went to the temple with everyone else at the special time for prayer.

 PEGBAG

'He'll never make it, poor little scrap,' said Kate's father. 'Look at him, all bones sticking out under his skin. He looks like a bag of clothes pegs.'

That's why Kate called him Pegbag. Her father, who bred

horses on his farm, told her not to bother giving him a name, because he wouldn't last long. But he did. The vet and her father encouraged Pegbag to feed, though at first he was too weak to stand. Kate stroked him and kept him warm and visited him every day, and as the weeks went by, the little foal grew stronger.

'He'll live,' said her father. 'But he'll never do a day's work. And he won't win prizes.'

'Can I keep him?' asked Kate anxiously.

'You'll have to do all the looking after him yourself,' he told her. 'I've no time.'

Every morning, early before school, Kate went down to the stables. She gave Pegbag some oats with vitamins to build him up, and she brushed his mane and tail. Then she led him out into the paddock where the other horses were grazing. He was still wobbly, but sometimes he pranced and kicked his legs as if he longed to run.

'Come on, Pegbag,' called Kate, dancing around him. 'You have to exercise. You have to grow strong.'

Then came the day when he galloped around the field, his neck stretched forward and hooves beating the ground, and she couldn't keep up with him. A year went by, and every day Kate would visit Pegbag, morning and evening. She would brush his coat till it shone and clean his hooves when he came in from the field. She talked to him, groomed him, exercised him and began to train him.

Her father was impressed. 'You've turned him into a champion,' he said. 'A couple more years, and you can begin to ride him.'

Some mornings when it was icy cold or she was tired from a late night, Kate would struggle to get out of bed. But then she thought of Pegbag calling to her as she drew near the stables, and she would force herself to get up. In the evenings he would hang his head over the gate, waiting for her to get back from school. With her father's help, she trained him and learnt to ride him around the fields and over the common.

One day, her father was working in the top field and trapped his arm under a log. All he could do was lie there calling out for help. It was Pegbag, out riding with Kate, who heard him, and he kept swerving towards the field. Kate could not understand what was happening, till she saw her father crouched over on the grass.

'Pegbag can help you,' she said. 'He's very strong.'

Her father explained how to tie a rope to the log, and then around the horse's shoulders. Straining with all his might, Pegbag pulled the log off her father and then carried him slowly back to the house.

'Pegbag, you're a winner!' said her father that night, standing in the horse's stall, his arm in a sling. 'And so are you, Kate. Both of you, a winning team.'

Pegbag snorted and moved his head towards Kate's outstretched hand. He crunched the peppermint she gave him and looked as if he agreed with every word.

PRAYER STEPS

Praying with a visual aid

Have a look at a diary or wall calendar. On your own or in a group, draw up a fictitious diary for one week. Write or draw in some of the things you do every day. Write or draw in some things you always mean to do, but you don't have the time. Write in the name of someone with whom you feel you need to be in contact more often. Take time to reflect on or discuss what you have written and drawn. Are you more likely to do something because you've written it down? What will you do about the person you've named? What stops you doing the things you mean to do? What might help you do them?

Praying with the Bible

Use the following passages for personal reflection or discussion.

* **Psalm 92:1–4:** What is the psalmist's attitude to praise and prayer? Do we think of praising and thanking God daily in our prayers?
* **Daniel 6:6–10:** What are the characteristics of Daniel's prayer life? What is his response to what he has heard? Do we put prayer first?
* **Luke 4:16–22:** What was Jesus brought up to do? How did it help him at this point in his ministry?
* **Acts 3:1–2:** What do we learn about Jewish custom and the custom of Peter and John? Do we have a custom of prayer?

Praying on your own

Try to make prayer a daily habit. Choose a time to which you know you can keep. There are many daily Bible reading notes that can help you, including BRF's *New Daylight* (see page 175 for further details, and visit www.biblereadingnotes.org.uk).

Praying in a group

When you come together as a group, get into the habit of having a time of prayer together. It doesn't have to be at the beginning or the end, but it helps if it can be at a regular stage in your meeting.

Praying it through

Draw your thoughts together in a time of quiet reflection, or use the appropriate version of the prayer below.

Each day of my life I pray to you, Lord.
Each day of my life, hear my prayer.

Each day of our lives we pray to you, Lord.
Each day of our lives, hear our prayer.

EMERGENCY!:
PRAYING IN A CRISIS

> **'When I was in trouble, Lord, I prayed to you.'**
> JONAH 2:2b

INTRODUCTION

Something happens. You don't know what to do. You may be frightened or confused. The only thing you can do is pray. You haven't got time to pray long and thoughtful prayers. You have only got time to call out to God.

Many people in the Bible turned to God when they were in trouble. In the Old Testament, Hezekiah had a threatening letter from a neighbouring king. He took it to the temple and asked God what he should do. Jonah called out to God when he was drowning. God sent a big fish to rescue him! In the Gospels, the disciples called to Jesus when they were on the lake in a storm. He stood up and calmed the sea.

In the book of Acts, as Stephen was dying, he called out to Jesus to welcome him into heaven.

 ## REDECORATING

Dr Penny was very popular and had many friends. He loved spending time with them, talking and laughing, and telling stories. A whole group would gather in his home and chat on a Friday evening. They would sit on the sofa or in armchairs or on the floor, anywhere where there was space, and then they would begin. First one would tell a story, then another would tell a joke. Someone might talk about a game they'd seen or an idea they'd had. No one was in a hurry to leave, and they would stay late into the night.

One morning, Dr Penny noticed that his sitting room was getting very shabby. The wallpaper was peeling, the sofa was sagging and broken, the carpet was covered in stains. 'Time to redecorate,' he said. He thought of asking his friends to help, but then he decided to do it all himself. 'No reason to trouble them. They're busy people.'

So Dr Penny went and bought some tins of paint and a roller. He chose new wallpaper and a new carpet. He carried home bags filled with glue and sticky tape, brushes and scrapers, and bottles of turps.

Monday night came, and Dr Penny began. It all needed to be ready by Friday, so he knew the sooner he started the better. The old wallpaper came off quite easily with the help of a steaming kettle. Patches of it fell off and stuck to the floor and the furniture. Dr Penny spent a long time scraping wallpaper off his shoes and in the end gave up and left it there.

'Now,' he said. 'A quick splash of paint on the ceiling and I can start putting up the new wallpaper.'

The paint splashed on more than the ceiling; it ran down the walls and covered the curtains and the old sofa. Some of it covered Dr Penny. His face and hands got stickier and stickier. 'Nearly finished,' he thought. 'Then I can have a bit of a clean-up.'

That was before he put his foot in the empty paint tin. His foot stuck. It seemed easier to leave it there and carry on, so Dr Penny laid out the new wallpaper and began to cover it with paste. His glasses were so flecked with paint that at first he didn't notice he was pasting the wrong side. 'Oh dear,' he said. 'I'll have to turn it over.'

But the wallpaper wouldn't turn over. Instead it curled up, round and round, with Dr Penny inside it. It wrapped him up till his arms were trapped by his side, and his body was one long column of paper. He looked like a huge toilet roll. At this point, Dr Penny realized he needed help. The problem was how to get to the phone. The easiest way seemed to be to lie on the ground and roll, which he did, picking up lots of bits of old wallpaper on the way. The phone was in the hall, which meant pushing down the door handle with his nose, and that wasn't pleasant.

It was a good thing Dr Penny had keyed in the numbers of his best friends so he only had to push one button to ring them. Again his nose came in useful. The first friend was out, but the second friend, Mrs Harris, answered. Dr Penny's face was half-wrapped in paper, but he managed to say one word, 'Help!'

'Who is that?' asked Mrs Harris. 'Dr Penny? Is that you?'

'Help!' cried Dr Penny, louder.

'I'm on my way,' she told him.

Mrs Harris came round, but she also brought lots of other friends with her. They weren't sure where to begin, but in the end they each took a different job and soon the worst of the mess was cleared up. Dr Penny came downstairs having had a very hot shower, and sat down with them in the kitchen.

'Reminds me of something that happened to me,' one of them said. And soon they were telling stories again, and laughing, and drinking tea, just as if it happened every day.

'See you on Friday, then,' they said as they left. 'We'll bring our overalls and get that room sorted.'

'Goodbye, friends,' called Dr Penny. 'See you on Friday.'

PRAYER STEPS

Praying with a visual aid

To do this you will need to know how to fold a paper dart. On your own or in a group, take a sheet of paper and write your name on it or a message to someone. You can colour it as well if you want. Try throwing the paper sheet. Now, fold the paper into a dart and send it across the room. Why did the paper fly better when it was folded? When would you need to send a message quickly to someone? When might our prayers be like the paper dart? Take time for personal reflection or shared discussion.

Praying with the Bible

Use the following passages for personal reflection or discussion.

* **2 Kings 19:9–19:** What did the letter say about God? How did Hezekiah respond? Is our first response to turn to God?
* **Jonah 2:1–9:** When did Jonah begin to pray, and how did God answer? In what sense can we all pray this prayer?
* **Luke 8:22–25:** How bad was the storm? Why did the disciples wake Jesus? What amazed them about him?

★ **Acts 7:54–60:** What caused such anger against Stephen? Why did they choose to stone him? What can we learn from his prayers?

Praying on your own

Are you worried, or do you not know what to do about something? Hezekiah brought a letter that was worrying him to God. Write or draw what is worrying you on a piece of notepaper and place it on the ground in front of you. Ask God to help you in this situation. If needed, find someone you trust to talk things through with.

Praying in a group

Divide into two teams. You have five minutes for each team to wrap one person from the other team in toilet paper (not over their face). When the five minutes is up, their own team members then have to unwrap them in the fastest time, without causing the wrapped person harm or distress. The winner is the first team to completely unwrap their team member. Finish by talking about how those who were wrapped up felt about being unwrapped and how those who were doing the unwrapping felt about helping to release their teammate.

Praying it through

Draw your thoughts together in a time of quiet reflection, or use the prayer below.

O Lord, hear my prayer.
When I call, answer me.

❖

SOAKED THROUGH: WHEN PRAYER AFFECTS OUR WHOLE LIFE

> **Never stop praying.**
> 1 THESSALONIANS 5:17

INTRODUCTION

We can pray at certain times; we can pray when we are in trouble; we can pray for other people. The Bible goes further and encourages us to pray all the time. This doesn't mean we never do anything else! It means that prayer accompanies everything we do. Life and prayer fit together.

In the Old Testament, Nehemiah and his helpers prayed at the same time as building the temple and keeping a lookout for their enemies. In the Gospels, Jesus encouraged his disciples never to give up praying for God's kingdom. In the book of Acts, the apostles decided that prayer as well as preaching was such an important part of their ministry that they needed to make sure they had enough time for it.

THE PRINCESS PORTRAIT

Toby tucked his sketchbook and canvas under his arm and climbed up the steps to the palace. He had climbed 142 steps before he reached the great doorway.

'I've come to paint the princess,' he gasped. 'I'm an artist.'

The door swung open and a guard waved him through. There were 35 more steps inside up to the room where the Princess Star would be sitting in a golden chair waiting to be painted. At least, the chair was there. But the princess had woken up in a bad mood and decided to go out riding on her horse instead.

'You can always paint the chair,' murmured a helpful lady-in-waiting.

'It's a start,' said Toby and set up his easel. He placed his canvas on the pegs and began sketching the chair, the room and the window. The window was large, taller than he was, and Toby's eye kept returning to it. He'd never seen the landscape from such a high position before, and he could see for miles. The hills were a soft, curving blue, like the surface of the sea. Light fell on fields speckled with green and gold, divided by green hedges. Dark trees decorated the hills like tiny skilful brush marks. Toby picked up his paintbrush to start working in his sketchbook.

'I'm so bored!' complained a loud but pretty voice. Toby turned and bowed as the beautiful Princess Star swept across the room and threw herself into the chair.

'Spangle, my horse, was being so difficult. And I caught my dress on a bramble. I'll have to throw it away.'

Toby stood in front of the easel and began drawing the princess.

'Let me see,' she said, jumping up after five minutes. 'Uh. You've made me look terrible. Can't you draw better than that?' She sat down again in a different position.

The lady-in-waiting rushed forward and smoothed her hair and dress. 'Just keep still, Your Highness,' she said. 'You want to look beautiful in your portrait, don't you?'

The princess gave a snort. 'I've had enough,' she said and ran out of the room.

'Come back tomorrow,' whispered the lady-in-waiting.

Toby could only bow once more, and then he turned back to his drawing through the window.

At home in his little room, Toby carried on painting the landscape from memory and began adding in some colour. He spent long hours trying to capture the light and the beauty he'd seen, sometimes forgetting to eat or sleep. Each day he would go to the palace. He would spend a little time painting the princess before she got bored and a long time painting through the window. At last the portrait was finished. The king and queen and several courtiers came into the room to see the painting. Toby lifted the cloth from the canvas and stood back. There were gasps of amazement and delight.

'It's so beautiful!' cried the queen, and the courtiers echoed, 'Yes, yes!'

'Jolly good,' said the king. 'View from the window, isn't it?'

'But where am I?' demanded the Princess Star. 'You were meant to be painting me!'

'She's right,' said the king. 'Where is the portrait?'

Toby lifted a second painting on to the easel. No one spoke for a while; they just stared at the portrait. Princess Star sat with her head slightly turned towards the window. Her eyes were as blue as the rolling hills, her skin was touched with the warm light of the sun, her hair was like soft fields of amber and gold, and her face had a beauty to it that was deep and strong.

'These paintings will hang side by side,' ordered the king in a firm voice. 'And then people will see how gazing on the beauty of the Princess Star helped you paint the landscape.'

Toby glanced over at the princess, and she lowered her eyes. She guessed that it was the hours he had spent painting the landscape that had helped him paint her. In that moment something happened to the princess. She decided, quite privately, that one day she really would look as beautiful as her portrait. She realized it would mean becoming beautiful on the inside, which would not be easy. But it would be worth it.

PRAYER STEPS

Praying with a visual aid

Light a scented candle or incense stick and let it burn for a while. Walk around and observe how the perfume fills the room. Do you like the smell? Does it influence your thoughts? Would you prefer it to be stronger or fainter? Has the room changed for you in any way? Reflect on or discuss your responses.

Praying with the Bible

Use the following passages for personal reflection or discussion.

✶ **Nehemiah 4:6–9**: How did Nehemiah and his companions cope with the hostility against them? Do we combine prayer and action as naturally as they did?

✳ **Luke 18:1–8:** What does this parable encourage us to do? How does our world compare with the world in the parable?

✳ **Acts 6:1–7:** What led to the apostles seeking more time for prayer and preaching? Did they ignore the problem or resolve it first? How can we make sure in our church that enough time is given to the right things?

✳ **1 Thessalonians 5:16–18:** What can we learn from these verses about prayer? How are we to think about Jesus?

Praying on your own

Pray about a place, a person, a situation or some part of your life that you have never prayed about before. See how prayer can naturally fit alongside everyday life.

Praying in a group

Take time to share news of things that are happening in the day-to-day life of your group, as well as concerns for the wider community, your church and the world.

Next, spend time praying for each other, encouraging people to pray aloud if they wish or in silence if they prefer.

Praying it through

Draw your thoughts together in a time of quiet reflection, or use the appropriate version of the prayer below.

Lord, may all I say and do be filled with prayer. Amen

Lord, may all we say and do be filled with prayer. Amen

NO REPLY: WHEN PRAYERS ARE NOT ANSWERED

> **I cry out day and night, but you don't answer.**
> PSALM 22:2a

INTRODUCTION

Among all the people who tell you about the wonderful answers to prayer they have received, there will be few who tell you when their prayers are not answered. We can easily feel that God is not answering our prayers, and we can be discouraged. We may even wonder if he really does care.

The Bible gives some examples of prayers that are not answered. James and John wanted to pray something cruel and violent, but Jesus would not let them. In Psalm 22, the writer cries out that God has deserted him and is not answering him. Yet the writer also looks forward to a time when God will hear his prayers and will bring salvation to the world. In his letter to the church in Corinth, Paul tells how he prayed for God to remove a problem he was having. But God answered in a different way. God replied that suffering made Paul weak, which allowed God's grace and power in his life to be even stronger. In the Gospels, Jesus went through the horrors of the cross, but he trusted that God would raise him from the dead.

For many reasons, we may have to go through unrelieved suffering, but we trust God to bring us to his kingdom one day.

PIRATES ABOARD

Marianne hid under the canvas and kept very still. The pirate was so close she could hear his rough breathing. She wanted to scream, but instead she bit hard on a piece of her dress. Although the ship was at anchor, it was rocking from side to side and lifting up and down until she thought she would be sick. The pirate moved away, and she heard a group of them go down to the lower deck. She was alone. If only she could get a message to her father, he would be sure to rescue her. He was close friends with the captain of a fine warship that could easily outrun the pirates.

Marianne waited till it was nearly dark, when the moon was bright enough for her to see where she was. Then she crept out from under the canvas and stood by the rails. She heard a man's footsteps, the padding of bare feet behind her, and she crouched down again into the shadows. When he had gone, she leant out over the rails and looked into the darkness below. Did she have the courage to drop down into the water and swim for shore? And then she saw a small rowing boat, bobbing way beneath her. A young man's face was lifted up, white in the moonlight. She recognized him: it was her brother, Alan. He held his finger to his lips to warn her to keep silent, and then he pointed to the shore. He would go for help—that is what he was telling her.

'Don't leave me,' she wanted to call out. But as the boat drew away, she wished it a safe journey. 'Don't be long.'

She remembered the moment the pirates had come on board—silent, deadly killers, knifing many of the sleeping passengers and crew. She remembered screams, and one man being hurled into the sea, his throat cut. She had crept into hiding then, and waited. She was sure the noise must have reached the shore, the cries for help, the shouts of anger and distress, and that people would be curious why a vessel waiting to sail should be so strangely disturbed. Yet nothing happened, and no one came—except Alan. Alan knew, that's what mattered. He knew that she was a prisoner and in danger. And he would tell her father. And surely her father would come to her rescue.

The tide had turned, and she could feel the waves slapping against the hull. The wind had picked up and was rattling the rigging. People were running along the deck, climbing, pulling at ropes and calling to each other in soft voices. And then the anchor was hauled up and the ship moved gently forward.

'No!' cried Marianne to herself in dismay. 'No! We can't be moving. Why does no one come?'

She peeped out from the canvas, and in place of the ship's own flag, she could see the Jolly Roger flying from the mast, a hideous human skull with two bones crossed beneath. She began to lose hope. No one would help. She was on her own. Hungry, thirsty and unhappy, she curled up in a tight ball and tried to sleep. The ship moved on towards the mouth of the estuary, and the pirates were in high spirits. Within an hour, they would be in the open sea. Once there, the whole ocean lay before them, and it would be hard for anyone to track them down.

Beyond the mouth of the estuary, further along the coast in a small bay, lay the warship, the *Avenger*, waiting...

PRAYER STEPS

Praying with a visual aid

On your own or in a group, look up at the sky. Can you see any stars? If not, does that mean they are not there? What are the reasons we might not see them? When can we see the stars most clearly? Reflect on or discuss how there are times we can see God's love more clearly and times we just need to trust him.

Praying with the Bible

Use the following passages for personal reflection or discussion.

* **Psalm 22:1–2:** Do these verses show a lack of faith? Or do they reflect confidence in God?
* **Luke 9:51–56:** What kind of Messiah did James and John think Jesus was? What did they feel about the Samaritans? What did they not understand?
* **2 Corinthians 12:7–10:** Why did God not answer Paul's request? What was Paul's response? Does this help us to cope if God does not answer our prayers?
* **James 4:1–4:** What did James observe about the reason people quarrel? How does this link with prayers not being answered? Do we use prayer to demand our own way?

Praying on your own

Close your eyes so that you are in darkness. Reflect on whether you are willing to trust God, regardless of whether your prayers are answered or not. If you are, raise your hands in front of you and clasp them together. Imagine you are holding on to God, even though you may not understand all that happens.

Praying in a group

Have some prayers of yours remained unanswered? How does this make you feel towards God? You may want to talk together as a group about this. Are you able to take a step towards God by talking to him about it?

Praying it through

Draw your thoughts together in a time of quiet reflection, or use the appropriate version of the prayer below.

I don't know why you have not answered my prayers. Help me to believe your power and love are still there for me. Amen

We don't know why you have not answered our prayers. Help us to believe your power and love are still there for us. Amen

✠

MAKING DEALS: CAN WE BARGAIN WITH GOD?

> **Simon… brought money and said to Peter and John, 'Let me have this power too!'**
> ACTS 8:18–19

INTRODUCTION

Sometimes we can be so desperate for God to answer our prayers that we try to think of ways to persuade him. We promise to do something we think he wants or to give him something precious to us, if only he will hear us. But what he wants from us is our commitment—that is, to trust him and follow him with all our hearts, not to bargain with him.

In the Bible, some people tried to make a deal with God for their own benefit. But God cannot be bought or bribed. For example, in Luke's Gospel, people came to Jesus, agreeing to follow him at a time that suited them. Jesus said 'no' as following him had to come first. In the book of Acts, a magician called Simon wanted to give the apostles money so that he could have the power of the Holy Spirit. They were shocked and told him he could not buy God's gifts.

In the Old Testament, however, Hannah so longed for a child that she wept in desperation. She promised to give her child to God's service if he heard her prayer. She was not bargaining with God but showing her commitment. God answered her prayer, and her son Samuel became a great prophet in Israel.

NOT FOR SALE

'Come on, young master. Come in and see the two-headed dog. Only a farthing.'

Richard dodged the man's arm and walked on between the stalls in the market. Around him were so many familiar sights and sounds and smells. On the same day every year the streets filled with traders, pedlars, sideshows and acrobats. Richard's father was the sheriff, responsible for making sure that there was no fighting and that stallholders were properly licensed.

A trader was selling hot chestnuts, cooking them over a charcoal fire. Richard bought some and munched as he walked along, spitting out the smoky bits. A young boy ran past, dodging through the crowd, his head bent low. Richard recognized one of his father's men chasing him. A group of laughing boys cheered on their friend, who had been spotted stealing an apple from a stall. At the top of the street, the more expensive traders were surrounded by richly dressed women and their servants. Richard peered through at colourful silks, silver jewellery decorated with beautiful blue stones, and mounds of strangely smelling spices all the colours of the earth. He imagined his mother wishing she were rich enough to buy such finery.

An argument began between a trader and a man in a long black robe. 'That's my price!' said the trader. 'It's a bargain. You won't see better wool than that this side of Kashmir.'

'I have seen better wool both sides,' said the man firmly. 'Yours is from a goat, and a sick goat at that. However, I'll take it for half the price.'

'Half!' shouted the trader. 'I suppose you'll want one of my legs to go with it! I can't come down more than a shilling.'

'Two.'

'A shilling and sixpence.'

Richard grinned and wandered down to the far end of the market. The road opened out to a field where livestock was being sold. He climbed on to a fence and watched people buying and selling or just enjoying a day out. A little apart from the crowd, his attention was caught by a bay mare, standing quietly with her head raised, her reins held by a very elderly man. Every line of her was beautiful, her coat glistened and her eye was clear and quick with life. Several people came up to the man, clearly wanting to buy from him. One by one they went away. She must be a high price, Richard thought. He slipped to the ground and walked over.

'How much?' he asked shyly.

'Not for sale.' The old man's voice was cracked with age.

Richard felt confused. 'I saw people bargaining with you. I'm sorry I misunderstood.'

'You like her?'

'Yes,' said Richard simply. 'She's the finest horse I've ever seen.'

The man laughed. 'You won't be any good at bargaining if you show such interest straight away.'

'But you said she's not for sale.'

The man reached up a hand and stroked the side of the mare's neck. 'No. She's not for sale. I trust this horse with my life. She's the best and brightest of them all, with a good nature and a quick mind. I can't sell her. What would a boy like you do with a horse like this?'

Richard explained that his father was the sheriff and kept his own horse in the stables and also a very old pony for his mother to ride. Soon Richard would begin working with his father, and he was on the lookout for a good horse. The old man gave Richard a hard look. Then he took the reins and looped them over Richard's arm.

'She's yours,' he said, shaking his head when Richard began to protest. 'No, no. I can't keep her any longer. I am too old. She needs to find a good home. People have tried to win her from me with money, tricks or promises. But you looked on her with love. Love doesn't buy and sell. She's my gift to you, if you will love her in return.'

As if in a dream, Richard walked back through the market, leading the bay mare. Through all the busy sounds his ears heard only one, the gentle rhythm of the horse's hooves behind him, striking against the stones.

PRAYER STEPS

Praying with a visual aid

Put a handful of coins on the table. On your own or in a group, make pencil rubbings so that several coins are shown on one sheet of paper. Underneath, draw something you would like to buy if you had enough money. Reflect or discuss how money influences us and how so much of our society is based on it. What power has money over you? What if you were offered a considerable sum? What matters to you more than money?

Praying with the Bible

Use the following passages for personal reflection or discussion.

* **Judges 6:36–40:** Did Gideon feel at ease asking God for a sign? Is there a better way to be sure of God's word?
* **1 Samuel 1:9–20:** Why did Hannah promise to give away what she most wanted to be given? Did she lose out?
* **Luke 9:57–62:** Is Jesus saying our home life is of no value in God's kingdom? On what terms were people willing to follow him? Do we try to make terms with God?
* **Acts 8:9–24:** Why was Simon's offer seen as so evil? What had he failed to understand about the nature of God? Is there any way we might make the same mistake?

Praying on your own

Have you decided to follow Jesus or are you still waiting for a better time? Jesus asks us to follow him just as we are. Maybe the right time for you is now.

Praying in a group

Talk about what you think God may want you to do as a group. Ask him to show you how you can follow him more closely.

Praying it through

Draw your thoughts together in a time of quiet reflection, or use the appropriate version of the prayer below.

Lord, thank you for your love that is freely given. I freely give my love to you. Amen

Lord, thank you for your love that is freely given. We freely give our love to you. Amen

✛

LETTING GO: TRUSTING GOD TO KNOW OUR NEEDS

> **'Your Father in heaven knows that you need all these.'**
> MATTHEW 6:32b

INTRODUCTION

It's easy to let something that's worrying us, or that we really want, take over our prayers. We keep on asking God to hear us and forget to let go and trust him. God already knows all that we need, and there may be other things we need to be praying about.

In the Old Testament, God met Elijah's needs even though Elijah prayed something quite different. In Matthew's Gospel, Jesus told his disciples not to worry about their lives. The important thing is to think about all that God is doing and wants us to do and trust the rest to him. In his letter to the church in Philippi, Paul said that he'd learnt to be satisfied with whatever he had and felt no need always to be chasing after more.

 ## I LIKE CABBAGE

The rabbit was famous for his parties. All the creatures were invited, however new they were to the garden. The caterpillar had been there only a week. She looked at her invitation and began to worry.

'Oh dear, I wonder what he will give us to eat. I ought to

drop by and just let him know that I only eat cabbage.' And she crawled away slowly across the grass.

'No problem!' said the rabbit, looking out from his burrow under the rhododendron bush. 'There are cabbages in the vegetable patch.'

'Thank you. That's kind. You see, I only eat cabbage.'

The rabbit checked after the caterpillar had gone, and yes, there were plenty of cabbages. 'I think I'll do a mixed salad,' he said to himself. 'There are radishes here, lettuces, cucumber. I must nip into the field for some corn. The birds will like that.'

When the rabbit arrived home from collecting the corn, there was a note in his letterbox. It was from the caterpillar. 'Just a reminder: I only eat cabbage.' The rabbit smiled and stored the corn in one of the rooms in his burrow.

The next day, the rabbit gathered blackberries for a great pie. He filled his basket to bursting and began dragging it home. A young frog jumped into his pathway and began to help him.

'Thank you, frog,' said the rabbit. 'Are you coming to my party?'

'You bet,' said the frog. 'Oh, I've a message for you from the caterpillar. She likes cabbage.'

'I know!' snapped the rabbit, who was feeling tired.

'I like flies,' said the frog. 'Don't worry, I'll bring my own.'

'Oh no, you don't have to do that,' said the rabbit more politely. 'I've ordered a dozen each for you and for the spider. Blue ones and green ones.'

'Can't wait!' called the frog, hopping away into the long grass.

The rabbit was just hauling the basket of blackberries down into his burrow, when a hedgehog hurried over. 'So glad I caught you,' she panted. 'The caterpillar particularly asked me to let you know that she only eats cabbage.'

'Thank you,' said the rabbit carefully and went in to lie down.

The day of the party came. The rabbit worked very hard preparing all the food. Friends arrived to help spread the food out on a large cloth on the grass. The party began, but there was no sign of the caterpillar. Everyone had a wonderful time, playing games and talking and eating as much as they liked.

As the sun began to set, the caterpillar crawled forward through the grass. She looked tired and upset. 'Oh rabbit,' she cried. 'I'm sorry I'm late. I got so worried about the cabbage, I couldn't find the party. I crawled to so many places, but there was no sign of you. I must have covered the whole garden.' She looked round and gave a cry of dismay. 'Oh, look, there's the cabbage. It's a beauty. You didn't forget. I should have trusted you. But now I'm too tired to eat anything.' And she curled up, right there on the grass, and fell asleep.

The next morning she woke up very hungry. All signs of the party had gone, and she was alone—but there on the grass next to her was the large juicy cabbage. She munched and munched with all her strength until she began to feel better. Then she went over to the rabbit's burrow.

'You're very kind,' she said. 'I really do feel better now. You see, I only eat...'

'I know!' said the rabbit. 'You only eat cabbage. For the moment.'

'What do you mean—for the moment?' asked the caterpillar in surprise.

'Wait and see,' smiled the rabbit, watching a white butterfly above his head sipping from the centre of a rhododendron flower. 'Wait and see.'

PRAYER STEPS

Praying with a visual aid

You will need a magnifying glass and a telescope or some binoculars. Alone or in a group, try looking at various objects through the magnifying glass. Then look at something as far away as you can with the telescope or binoculars. Did you see the magnified objects in a new way? Did you spot something new about them? When you looked through the telescope or binoculars, did objects appear closer than before? Take time to reflect or discuss how we see life from a limited viewpoint, and how God sees and knows us.

Praying with the Bible

Use the following passages for personal reflection or discussion.

* ★ **1 Kings 19:1–9:** What state was Elijah in when he prayed? What did he pray? In what ways did God meet Elijah's needs, physical and spiritual?
* ★ **Matthew 6:25–34:** Was Jesus suggesting the material world doesn't matter? How can we be free from everyday worries? How can we think more about God's kingdom without losing touch with reality?

✴ **Philippians 4:10–20:** What is Paul's attitude to his own comfort and conditions? What has he discovered that helps him? What is his prayer for the Philippians and how does he respond to their gifts?

✴ **1 Timothy 6:6–10:** What are the basic needs Paul mentions? Are we content with what we have? How can that contentment be attained?

Praying on your own

Is there something that you keep praying for and worrying about at the same time? Take a pebble in your hand, grip it very hard, and then gradually let go of it and put it on the floor in front of you. Say the prayer below or your own prayer.

Praying in a group

Have a pile of stones or pebbles in front of you. Is there something that you are worrying about or that you keep thinking about? Take one of the stones and hold it very hard. Let the stone be whatever is on your mind. Then gradually let go of it as if you were handing it over to God. Say the prayer below together as a group.

Praying it through

Draw your thoughts together in a time of quiet reflection, or use the appropriate version of the prayer below.

Father, as I let go of this stone, I want to let go of all that is worrying me. Help me to trust you for all that I need.

Father, as we let go of these stones, we want to let go of all that is worrying us. Help us to trust you for all that we need.

BLESSING AND CURSING: PRAYING WHEN PEOPLE DO WRONG THINGS

> **'Ask God to bless anyone who curses you.'**
> LUKE 6:28a

INTRODUCTION

When you declare you want something good to happen to someone else, it means you are blessing them. When you want them to suffer or fail in some way, you are cursing them.

The Bible is full of people blessing and cursing each other. Often people would curse their enemies, hoping for them to fail. Jesus told his disciples to bless other people, even the ones who were cursing them. It is hard to ask God to bless people who are not treating us well. But blessing people can change a bad situation into a good one. Blessing people can bring God's goodness and love into your life and their lives.

 COMPOST

Margarita Penfeather was a wonderful gardener. Her beautiful garden was filled with prize-winning flowers and vegetables. Rain or shine, she would be outside, carefully cutting away a dead stalk, tugging out a weed or tying up a dahlia. She fed her garden with special compost, which she had put together to her own recipe—and the flowers loved it. They would bloom bigger and brighter and better than anyone else's around.

Next door, Phil Potter loved gardens, but he did not see himself as a good gardener. Phil thought that gardens on the whole should look after themselves. He believed his flowers grew no matter how little he fussed over them. 'Yes, I have a bit of greenfly,' he would say, 'but the ladybirds eat them. And I don't mind slugs and snails. The thrushes eat the snails. And black slugs help break up the dead leaves.'

Margarita in her worst moments would throw any snails she found into Phil's garden, but they would crawl right back again, so she was forced to drown them in cider. Margarita loathed Phil, and Phil didn't much like Margarita. If they were both in the garden at the same time, they wouldn't speak to each other.

But then, something very unpleasant happened. One by one, Margarita's flowers began to turn yellow and die.

'Someone has put weedkiller on them!' she screeched. 'It's that man next door. I know it is. He's jealous, and now he's murdered my flowers!' And in a rage she bought a whole can of weedkiller and sprayed it all over the plants in Phil's garden. Within hours, both gardens were looking very sorry for themselves.

'You know you are completely mad!' cried Phil over the fence. 'I never touched your garden.' He went inside and slammed the door. Now, Phil had a friend who was a scientist. While Margarita was out shopping, Phil climbed over the fence and dug out a dead flower and a tub of soil. He sent them to his friend so that the soil could be analyzed to see what was wrong with it. The scientist sent back his report. By mistake, some harmful chemicals had got into Margarita's special compost and were killing the plants. The chemicals would not stay long in the soil, so the flowers could be replanted the next season.

Phil struggled within himself. It would be so easy not to tell Margarita, easy to let her go on using her compost so that her plants would keep on dying. But Phil couldn't do it; he loved gardens too much. Finally, he left a message on Margarita's answer phone telling her the compost was the problem.

Margarita was quiet for a few days, but then she sent a note saying, 'Thank you.'

The following spring, as they planted new seedlings in their gardens, Phil and Margarita began to talk to each other. A few words to start with, but after a while they were chatting away about flowers and the best way to grow them.

'Have some of my new compost,' Margarita offered. 'There's enough for both gardens.'

'And no more weedkiller?' Phil asked her.

'No more weedkiller,' said Margarita.

PRAYER STEPS

Praying with a visual aid

Alone or in a group, shake some salt from a salt cellar into the palm of your hand. Taste the salt. When is salt a good thing? What happens if our bodies need salt? When is it healing? When does it become bad for us? Think about the saltiness of the sea. Think about tears. Take time for personal reflection or shared discussion.

Praying with the Bible

Use the following passages for personal reflection or discussion.

* **Deuteronomy 11:26–32:** What was the choice given to the Israelites? Do we think of God blessing and cursing, or only blessing? What is the result of God's curse on something?
* **Luke 6:27–36:** How might we sum up the message of these verses? How were the disciples to be different from other people? Do those who follow this teaching still stand out as different today?
* **Romans 12:14–21:** How do these verses echo the verses from Luke? What is the warning in verse 21?
* **Galatians 3:10–14:** Look at these verses alongside the Deuteronomy reference. How did Christ rescue us from the curse of God's broken laws? What is the blessing we can now receive?

Praying on your own

Think of someone you are finding difficult. Picture them in your mind and then say the words of the blessing written below. (If the person you are thinking of has hurt you very much, you might want to talk to someone you trust to help you sort it out.)

Praying in a group

Arrange some tea lights around a lighted candle on a metal tray. In a time of silence, each of you light a tea light for someone as a sign of blessing. It may be someone you feel good about, or someone you are finding difficult. Take a moment to think about that person, and ask God to bless them. You can use the words of the blessing written below.

Praying it through

Draw your thoughts together in a time of quiet reflection, or use the prayer below, which is a blessing from Philippians 4:23.

I pray that our Lord Jesus Christ will be kind to you and will bless your life!

DELIVER US FROM EVIL: ASKING GOD TO PROTECT US

> Put on all the armour that God gives, so you can defend yourself against the devil's tricks.
>
> EPHESIANS 6:11

INTRODUCTION

Prayer is an important way of fighting evil. We can ask God to protect us and other people against evil powers.

In the Old Testament, Moses prayed while the Israelites went to war, and while his hands were raised, they kept winning. This picture reminds us how prayer helps us in times of struggle. In John's Gospel, Jesus prayed for his followers, not that they would be safe from danger in this world, but safe from anything evil that might destroy their relationship with him. In his letter to the Ephesians, Paul tells us we are not fighting other people, but we are in a battle against spiritual forces that are disobeying God. We must keep on praying, especially for others.

 ## THE STORM

Petra woke early, her mother shaking her. 'Get your brother,' she said. 'We must hurry.'

Petra's father was already outside, talking in a low voice to a group of men. By the first light of dawn Petra could make out figures coming from the various houses, holding on to children or carrying babies. She pulled Carl out of bed and laid a hand over his mouth to warn him to be quiet.

'You'll need this,' said her mother, handing her a kitchen knife.

'What for?' asked Petra.

'In case...' her mother didn't finish.

Petra knew it was all she had with which to defend herself. They were escaping from enemy soldiers who had entered their land, taking over all the towns and villages. Some people had fled to the fields trying to escape over the border, but they had been cut down by the soldiers. Others had given in and joined the enemy's forces, only to become little more than slaves.

The small party headed for the mountains. They had little hope of crossing over to freedom, but they were determined to survive and fight on as long as they could. They were armed with all the weapons they possessed; even the children carried axes and knives. Everywhere there were signs of the enemy gaining ground. They were burning the land between the villages, so that thick smoke hung in the air and stung their eyes.

Petra hung on to her brother's hand as they crossed the open ground towards the mountain ranges. After hours of walking and climbing up through the mountains, the villagers were hungry and cold, but they knew they must not stop for long. As they rested, Petra's dad went ahead to see the best way forward. 'It's no use,' he said, returning. 'There's a deep ravine ahead of us, with sheer sides down into the darkness. We'll have to turn back.'

'We can't,' said Stefan, the leader of their village. 'The soldiers have reached the mountains. We have no choice. We must stay here and fight. Let the children go forward as far as they can.'

The children moved along the edge of the ravine and then gathered in a huddle, as far down the path as they could go. Their parents turned towards the oncoming enemy and prepared to fight till all lives were lost.

'If only we had a bridge,' wailed Sonya, Petra's friend. 'Then we could get to the other side.'

The children looked across the ravine. It was not wide, but it was too far to jump.

'We need a rope,' said Petra.

Carl was more interested in the rock face behind them. A single tall tree grew deep in a crevice between the rocks, its roots curling up out of the soil. 'Tree,' he pointed.

'Of course!' cried Sonya. 'The tree would make a bridge.'

'Come on,' said Mark, who was the oldest. 'This is our chance!'

They began to hack at the base of the tree, slowly chipping away with their knives and axes. The smallest children could only reach the roots, but they worked away at it with all their strength. Meanwhile, their parents waited for the soldiers to approach.

'We'll never do it,' the children said to each other, exhausted. 'We need help.'

'Come on,' Mark urged them. 'We mustn't stop. We've got no choice.'

Like sounds of battle, the sound of their blows hammered

out in the gathering darkness. And then it began to rain, heavy drops, threatening the kind of storm you get only in the mountains. The children were drenched within seconds. The wind started to blow, hurtling through the ravine like the roar of a great animal. The enemy soldiers, confident they need not hurry, dropped some way back among the rocks to find shelter.

Suddenly there was a great crash, and a brilliant streak of lightning shot out of the sky, hitting the tree. The wind blew against its wounded trunk, and the tree groaned and fell forward across the ravine.

'A bridge! It's a bridge!' cried the children. Carefully, Mark tested that the tree was secure. Petra ran back and pulled at her mother's hand. Together, the whole party crossed over, one by one. On the far side they heaved the tree forward so that it crashed downwards into the ravine.

'We're safe!' breathed Stefan. 'We can go down into the valley and start new lives. But we mustn't forget. We won't give in until our land is free again.'

'The children saved us,' said Petra's mother. 'They brought the tree down with their axes.'

'It was the wind and lightning,' said Petra. But the truth was, it was both.

PRAYER STEPS

Praying with a visual aid

On your own or in a group, find or draw some objects we use to protect ourselves, such as Wellington boots, gardening gloves, sun glasses, plastic visor, cycle helmet. Think about the objects. From what do they protect us? Take time for personal reflection or shared discussion. How can we protect our minds as well as our bodies? What can protect our relationship with God?

Praying with the Bible

Use the following passages for personal reflection or discussion.

* **Exodus 17:8–13**: What was the significance of Moses' arms raised to heaven? Why did the Israelites need to see Moses praying? Does it help to know people are praying for us?
* **John 17:15–19**: What does Jesus pray for his disciples? In what way does he pray they will be safe? Does this mean they will never get hurt?
* **Ephesians 6:10–18**: Where is the battle taking place? Is the outcome in any doubt? How does the armour of God and prayer go together?
* **Revelation 12:7–12**: What do we learn from this image of Michael and the angels fighting the dragon? How did the dragon fight God's people? How were they able to defeat it?

Praying on your own

Find out about some organization working to bring aid. Read through their literature and see if you want to support them and pray for them.

Praying in a group

As a group, think how you can work for God's kingdom, in action and in your prayers. How about supporting an aid organization or Fairtrade or a local community project?

Praying it through

Draw your thoughts together in a time of quiet reflection, or use the appropriate version of the prayer below.

Father, help me to work for what is good and protect me from evil. Amen

Father, help us to work for what is good and protect us from evil. Amen

GIVE US STRENGTH!:
PRAYING FOR HELP TO DO
WHAT IS RIGHT

'I have prayed that your faith will be strong.'
LUKE 22:32b

INTRODUCTION

Prayer can help us when we are struggling to do what is right. We can also pray for other people to help them to be strong.

In the Old Testament, Adam and Eve did what they knew was wrong. As a result, they became afraid of God, and hid from him. Psalm 1 tells us that if we do what God wants, we will be like a strong tree that always produces fruit and is full of life. In Luke's Gospel, Jesus prayed for Peter that he would not give up following him. Peter went on to be a very important Christian leader in the church.

 ## TREES AND SNAKES

Either the narrator can read all the words, or the other parts can be spoken by the players.

Cast:
Narrator
Group of snakes
Oak tree
Silver birch tree

The two trees stand with their arms up and fingers outstretched.
You can move and sway if you want, but don't move your feet.
It's easier if you keep your arms slightly bent. The snakes begin to
gather around the trees, hissing.

Narr: Two trees stood by the riverbank; their roots grew
deep into the soil. One was an oak tree, the other
a silver birch. They were strong and healthy. But
some snakes arrived, and they thought it would be
fun to make the trees fall over.
First of all, the snakes said to the trees:

Snakes: If you get out of the ground and move, you will
be much happier. You'll be just like us, and we
will think much better of you. You can join us and
be our friends.

Narr: But the oak tree said:

Oak: No, we are not like snakes, we are trees, and we're
not meant to take our roots out of the ground. If
we do, we will die.

Narr: The snakes began to get angry and hissed loudly.
One snake was very poisonous and s/he said:

Reproduced with permission from *Tales for the Prayer Journey* published by BRF 2007 (978 1 84101 509 5)
www.barnabasinchurches.org.uk

Snake: I'm going to make you move. I shall flick poison into your branches and force you to move. *(The snake flicks his/her fingers at the tree.)*

Narr: But the silver birch said:

Birch: You can poison our leaves till they wither and fall, but we won't move.

Narr: Then all the snakes joined ends till they'd made a long rope. And they said:

Snake: We'll pull you over, we're very strong.

The snakes hold hands in a circle around the trees and pull first to the left, then to the right.

Narr: But the oak tree said:

Oak: We are much stronger than you because our roots go very deep into the ground and keep us firm.

Narr: However hard the snakes pulled, the trees stayed upright. Then the snakes tried something else. They started laughing:

Snakes: Ha ha ha ha ha! You're a silly tree. You can't move, you can't move. Ha ha ha.

Narr: But this time the trees didn't answer the snakes at all. They just ignored them until the snakes went quiet.

   Now, one of the snakes was very clever, and s/he spoke with a bit of a sneer. S/he said:

Snake: Of course, only *sad* trees can't move. Sad trees are just stuck in their ways. You can tell a tree is cool when it can move.

Reproduced with permission from *Tales for the Prayer Journey* published by BRF 2007 (978 1 84101 509 5)

www.barnabasinchurches.org.uk

Narr: This was too much for the silver birch tree. S/he so wanted to be cool. And so s/he tugged and tugged at her/his roots till one by one they came out of the ground with a pop. *(Silver birch tree lifts feet one by one.)* The oak tree cried out to her/him to stop:

Oak: Stop! Stop! If you pull your roots out, you'll die. Look at that dead grass on the ground. You'll be just like that. You'll blow away on the wind.

Narr: Just in time, the silver birch remembered s/he needed her/his roots in order to live. S/he pushed them back into the soil, and stood up straight. At this point the snakes got bored. They went away, hissing, and left the trees standing there, their roots firmly planted in the soil.

Snakes sit back down. Trees stand for a moment and then sit down too.

PRAYER STEPS

Praying with a visual aid

You will need a good pot plant and a handful of loose grass or leaves. On your own or in a group, take a hairdryer and direct it at the pot plant and then at the grass or leaves. What do you notice? Why do the leaves fly about? Why does the pot plant stay upright? Is it because of the pot? Or because of what is growing under the soil? Take time for personal reflection or shared discussion.

Praying with the Bible

Use the following passages for personal reflection or discussion.

* **Genesis 3:1–8:** How did the snake deceive Adam and Eve? What did they find tempting? What did they do wrong?
* **Psalm 1:** Think of the difference between trees and straw. In what ways can we make sure we are like the trees?
* **Luke 22:31–34:** What struggle do we see in these verses going on in the spiritual world? Do we pray for people that they will remain strong? Or would we rather condemn them?
* **1 Corinthians 10:12–13:** Are we overconfident? How can we be strong and yet remain aware of the dangers? Have you known a time when God showed you how to escape from temptation?

Praying on your own

Just as Jesus prayed for his friend Peter, pray for someone you know who is finding faith difficult, or for someone who needs strength to do what is right.

Praying in a group

Some or all of you act out the sketch about the trees and snakes. At the end, pray for each other that you will be strong like the trees and not give in to what the snakes are saying. What sort of things might the snakes be saying in our lives?

Praying it through

Draw your thoughts together in a time of quiet reflection, or use the appropriate version of the prayer overleaf.

Dear Lord, please make me strong when I am tempted to do what is wrong. Help me to be like a tree so that I can stand firm. Amen

Dear Lord, please make us strong when we are tempted to do what is wrong. Help us to be like the trees so that we can stand firm. Amen

ON THE MOUNTAINTOP:
SPECIAL PLACES FOR PRAYER

> On the Sabbath we went outside the city gate to a place
> by the river, where we thought there would be a Jewish
> meeting place for prayer.
> ACTS 16:13

INTRODUCTION

Does it matter where we pray? Do we have to pray in church? Doesit help to have one place where we pray? We can pray anywhere, anytime, but sometimes a special place can help us focus on God. Some Christians today make a special space for prayer in their homes or their rooms.

In the Old Testament, Solomon built the temple where people could pray, or if they were far away, they could turn towards it and pray. In the Gospels, Jesus often went up into the mountains to pray. In the book of Acts, when Paul and Luke wanted to preach to the Jewish community in Philippi, they went to the riverside, looking for the place of prayer.

 ## THE TREE HOUSE

Jake's dad knocked on his bedroom door. 'Are you in there, Jake?' he called softly.

Jake lifted his head from his knees where he was crouching on the bare floor. 'No,' he said.

'We have to go, Jake. Come on, it's time to say goodbye. Your mum and Sophie are already in the car.'

Jake walked one last time around the room, his arms pressing against the walls. He knew every patch and mark in the plaster, every hole in the skirting board. He looked through the window at the small patch of lawn with the wild bit at the end where there were stinging nettles. He'd lived in this house all his life, and now they were moving.

'I don't want to go,' he wailed to himself.

The new house was in a different town, and he and his little sister would have to go to a new school and make new friends. Jake's new bedroom was bigger than his last one, but he didn't care. He looked out of the window of his new bedroom at the sky and wished he could go home. His real home. He noticed an old tree at the bottom of the garden, leaning slightly and pushing the fence out into a curve. Halfway up the tree, Jake could see a bundle of sticks and rags wedged among the branches and wondered what it was.

Tripping over packing cases and boxes, he managed to get out through the back door. The garden was very overgrown with bushes and trails of brambles. Jake waded through the long grass to get to the tree and looked up. What he'd seen was the remains of an old tree house, rotting and broken, with bits of faded carpet sticking through the planks.

'A tree house?' said his dad. 'That sounds fun. Why don't we mend it?'

Over the next few weeks, Jake worked hard. He began to make friends at school, and some of them came round to join him. Jake's dad helped, sawing pieces of wood and making sure the house was firmly fixed. It only needed a rope ladder and a square of carpet, and then it was ready. Jake carried up a wooden box with a lid to keep things in and to use as a table. His mum gave him some old cushions and a rug.

Every day Jake climbed up to the tree house after school, often with his new friends.

'Mum's decorating,' he told them gloomily. 'It's safer in here.'

Sometimes the tree house became a powerful place where adventures happened, and they were surrounded by evil creatures trying to attack them. Sometimes it flew them to new worlds, through space and time. Sometimes they just sat and talked about things. And sometimes Jake was there on his own, reading, doing his homework or just dreaming.

His dad teased him. 'You're in there so much we could rent out your room.'

'You'll be sleeping in there next,' said his mum. And then, when she saw his face, she guessed what was coming.

'A sleepover!' cried Jake. 'Great idea, Mum! I'll call the others.'

His parents looked at each other. 'Who's on night duty?' asked his mum.

'It was your idea,' said his dad.

'I don't like spiders,' said his mum.

Jake left them to it and went upstairs to get his sleeping bag and phone his friends.

PRAYER STEPS

Praying with a visual aid

On your own or in a group, look at some door keys. Imagine one of them is your front door key or use your own. What is special about your front door key? What does it mean to have a house to live in, a place to belong? What makes your home different from other homes you visit? What would you like to see in your home that you feel is missing? Take time for personal reflection or shared discussion.

Praying with the Bible

Use the following passages for personal reflection or discussion.

* **1 Kings 8:27–30:** What does Solomon understand about God? What is he asking God to do? How can we be careful not to think that God only belongs in one place?
* **Matthew 14:22–23:** What was special for Jesus about the mountainside? Why did he send the disciples and the crowds away?
* **Acts 10:9:** Peter was staying with a man called Simon in Joppa. The rooftop would have been flat. Why did Peter go on the rooftop to pray? What time of day was it? What would it have been like?
* **Acts 16:13:** Philippi was a Roman city. Why did the Jews living there meet by the riverside to pray? Where would they normally have met to pray?

Praying on your own

You may like to find a special place to pray, indoors or outdoors. It helps if it is a peaceful place, free of noise and clutter. God often speaks to us through the Bible, so take one with you.

Praying in a group

Make a prayer place. Use coloured cushions or wooden benches to sit on. Keep a Bible there. You can use objects, paintings, photos or a cross to help you pray, or you can keep it very simple. If you need to pack it away after each session, keep a special bag or box to put things in.

Praying it through

Draw your thoughts together in a time of quiet reflection, or use the appropriate version of the prayer below.

Lord, bless this place where I pray. Help me to meet you here. Amen

Lord, bless this place where we pray. Help us to meet you here. Amen

AMEN!: MEETING WITH OTHERS FOR PRAYER

> The apostles often met together and prayed with a single purpose in mind.
> ACTS 1:14

INTRODUCTION

When we pray with a group of people, it is not because we are trying to put more pressure on God. Praying together unites us and turns us towards him. God wants us to be in agreement with each other, and with him, in our prayers. If we agree with a prayer we've heard, we can say 'amen' at the end of it. Amen means something like 'let it be so'.

In the Old Testament, Esther asked the Jewish people to spend time praying for her while she risked her life for them. As we agree in our prayers together, Jesus has promised to be with us and to hear us. The first disciples often prayed together and agreed with each other's prayers.

 ## BRIDGET THE BEAVER

'Look out!' yelled Bridget as the tree crashed to the ground, scattering the other beavers.

'You're meant to shout "timber",' grumbled her sister Bessie and went back to gnawing through the bark of a sapling.

Bridget tugged and pushed the tree towards the canal.

Another beaver was in the way, and the canal was already jammed with tree trunks.

'This is hopeless,' Bridget complained. She dragged the tree across the ground and rolled it into the canal further down.

The tree went a little way and then stuck against something.

'What are you doing!' cried Bridget, as a head came up out of the water.

'Building a dam,' muttered the beaver.

'But it's a canal! You can't build a dam across a canal! Canals are for carrying things down to the river!' Bridget was hopping and thumping her tail in anger.

The beaver climbed out on to the bank, dripping. 'No one to stop me,' he said.

Other beavers came up and began arguing. Bridget's cousin Ferdie walked past, carrying a large stone in his front paws. 'I've started building a house,' he said. 'Come and see.'

Bridget followed him down to the river. There were beavers everywhere, all of them building dams and lodges and storehouses. Bridget could see the beginnings of at least six dams. Ferdie showed her a mound he'd started. 'This is my house,' he said proudly. Then he looked a bit puzzled. 'It seems to have got smaller.'

They watched as two beavers swam up and helped themselves to sticks and bark from the mound.

'No!' cried Ferdie. 'Stop! That's my house!'

'No point in building it there,' said one of the beavers. 'With dams either side, you'll be nowhere near the water.'

Bessie came along with two of their younger brothers,

dragging the sapling between them. 'Room for another dam in there, I think,' she said and plopped into the water next to Ferdie's house.

Ferdie threw the stone down in dismay. 'This is hopeless!' he said. 'It's just a waste of time. I give up.' He sat down and started combing his fur with his claws, ignoring everything around him. Bridget chewed on a juicy piece of stick and thought hard.

'The trouble is,' she said, 'we all want the same things, but we're not working together.'

It was midnight, and the moon shone brightly down on a large gathering of beavers. The word had passed round that there was a meeting and that Bridget had something to say. Bridget began: 'We all need houses. We all need shelter from the cold. We all need somewhere safe to hide from bears and wolves. We all need deep water where we can store our food. We all need to build dams to keep the water deep enough. But we need something else, too. We need to work together. We need to agree on things. It's not going to happen any other way.'

The beavers nodded. They'd all been feeling something like that. One of the older beavers stood on his hind legs. 'She's right,' he said. 'Let's do it!'

They began to talk about the best way to get things done. They decided they only needed one dam to make a wide, deep lake, and they could all help to build that. Whole families could live in one house and share the food store. As they talked, Bridget began to see a picture in her mind of beavers building and working together, agreeing with each other, asking for help when they needed it, warning each other when danger was near. It all seemed to make good sense.

Before long, the beavers had got so used to working together, they couldn't remember a time when they'd lived any other way. And the homes and dams and lakes and canals they built kept them safe and warm and well fed, winter and summer, year after year.

PRAYER STEPS

Praying with a visual aid

Alone or in a group, take a length of thick string. Tug at the two ends to see if you can break it. Cut off a short section and start to unravel the string. Pick at it until you are left with just a pile of fibres. Can you break the fibres at all? How were the fibres joined together? Are you surprised how strong the fibres became as a piece of string? Take time for personal reflection or shared discussion.

Praying with the Bible

Use the following passages for personal reflection or discussion.

✷ **Esther 4:8–17**: How did Esther act on behalf of her people? How did Mordecai challenge her? What part did prayer have in this?

✷ **Matthew 18:19–20**: On what condition will God answer prayer? Do we see this happening when we pray? Are we aware of Jesus being with us?

✷ **Luke 24:28–35**: What caused the two disciples to recognize Jesus? How did the presence of Jesus transform them? Why did they go straight to the apostles?

✱ **Acts 1:14:** What do we learn of the early church community from this verse? How can we become a similar community?

Praying on your own

Think of the people you know who pray for you. Ask God to bless them in turn.

Praying in a group

Play a game like charades in two teams, where you have to work out together what each of your team is going to do. In the same way, praying together is like working as a team. End with a time of group prayer.

Praying it through

Draw your thoughts together in a time of quiet reflection, or use the appropriate version of the prayer below.

Lord, thank you for the times I can pray with other people. Amen

Lord, thank you for the times we can pray with other people. Amen

HERE I AM, LORD:
ALONE WITH GOD

> **'When you pray, go into a room alone and close the door.'**
> MATTHEW 6:6

INTRODUCTION

Praying on our own may seem difficult—we might prefer to be with our friends. But being with God is like being with a friend, so we are not really alone. Praying alone means we can say what comes into our minds, we can say private things, we can seem much closer to God, and God may speak to us in a special way.

In the Old Testament, Isaiah stood alone before God and was given a vision and a special ministry. In the Gospels, Jesus often looked for somewhere he could pray alone and taught his disciples to do the same. In the book of Acts, Paul spent time on his own after he had met Jesus, deepening his relationship with God and learning from him.

 ## YOU AT THE BACK THERE!

'Keep still at the back there!' commanded Grandma Rumble, the oldest elephant.

Benjie waved his ears and shuffled his feet and tried not to move. He'd managed to sneak a banana from the tree just behind him, but Grandma Rumble had noticed.

His sister Nettle gave him a push and he pushed back. Their mother turned round and glared at them. Benjie had been known as 'you at the back there' ever since he'd been born. He'd always kept in the crowd and never got too close to Grandma Rumble, and because of her weak eyes, she couldn't see who he was.

Grandma Rumble was giving her favourite talk about the importance of fresh water and how if they didn't find water soon they'd have to move on and how her sister's herd, who lived nearby, would have to move with them. Benjie half listened, but he didn't really think it had anything to do with him. He saw his cousin, Chip, at the far end of the line, waiting to dash off and wallow in the mud pool. Benjie edged closer to him. Grandma Rumble finished her speech with a good strong trumpet, and all the elephants broke away and began eating again.

The mud pool was drying out fast around the edges, and the centre was too shallow for the adult elephants. Benjie, Chip and Nettle waded in. They sucked up mud in their trunks and sprayed it all over their skin. Aah, it was so cool and comfortable. The flies that had been bothering them landed on a layer of mud instead of skin and flew off to bother someone else.

'Come on, you at the back there!' laughed Chip. 'Let's eat all the leaves on that bush.'

Nettle shook her ears. 'I can't believe Grandma Rumble doesn't know who you are.'

'I like it this way,' said Benjie. 'I don't bother her, and she doesn't bother me. I go where the herd goes, and I do what the herd does. That's all I need to do.'

'She tells me stories sometimes,' said Nettle. 'Stories of the old days when she was young. There were loads more trees then. And it rained more.'

Benjie couldn't imagine Grandma Rumble telling stories. She seemed far too stern and bossy. She was always telling everyone to keep still, and he found that very difficult to do.

Benjie soon got tired of eating leaves and wandered off to find something juicier, a nice piece of fruit perhaps. Standing under a tree, he curled up his trunk to smell what was growing on it. A very deep voice behind him said softly, 'Benjie!'

Benjie jumped and turned round. Grandma Rumble was standing there, looking straight at him.

'Y-yes?' he said.

'Benjie, it's time you and I had a talk. Come for a walk with me.'

Together they walked through the trees a little way from the herd. Grandma Rumble talked. She talked about the time when as a boy elephant he would have to leave the herd and join the other males. She talked about the dangers he would face. She told him a horrible story about how some of her family had been killed by poachers and how he should always be on the lookout for them. She also told him that if ever he needed to talk to her, she'd be there.

Then Grandma Rumble asked Benjie some questions, and soon he was talking. Not much at first, but then more and more. He found he was enjoying himself. She seemed very interested in him and his friends. And she laughed when he told her how he'd played a trick on Chip. He'd never known Grandma Rumble could laugh.

Then she asked him to do something. 'It's very important,' she said. 'You and your friends are old enough now, and your tusks are strong enough. I want you to start digging for water. If you find water, you will do a great service to the herd. Will you do this?'

'Yes,' said Benjie. 'I will.'

'Good. Well, I've enjoyed our chat. I look forward to another.' Grandma Rumble plodded off through the trees, her great ears flapping a goodbye.

'What are you doing?' asked Nettle, seeing him wandering deeper into the forest.

'Digging for water,' said Benjie. He sniffed at the ground with his trunk. 'It's here. I know it is. Come on, it's very important. You, too, Chip,' he called to his cousin.

In the end, the water hole they dug supplied the herd for many years to come. Their sister herd joined them, and other animals came and drank gratefully.

'You at the back there!' trumpeted Grandma Rumble as the herd lined up before her.

'Yes, you. Benjie. And friends. Thank you. Well done. We're very proud of you.'

Nettle shoved him from one side and Chip from the other. But for once, Benjie didn't move.

PRAYER STEPS

Praying with a visual aid

Have some paper ready and water-based ink or paint. On your own or in a group, cover your thumb with ink or paint and then press it on to the paper to record your fingerprint. Try with both thumbs and all your fingers. Are any the same? Is there anyone else with your fingerprints? What other methods are used to identify people these days? Reflect or discuss what it feels like to be unique, to have no one the same as you. How does this make you feel about yourself? How does it affect the way you see your relationship with God?

Praying with the Bible

Use the following passages for personal reflection or discussion.

* **Isaiah 6:1–8**: How did Isaiah feel in the presence of heavenly beings? How did God respond to him? How did he answer God?
* **Matthew 6:5–6**: What is the contrast between the two ways of praying? Are we too interested in what other people think of us? Do we 'pray and display'?
* **Luke 5:15–16**: What can we learn here about prayer? Do we have a place to which we go to be alone? Do we find being alone difficult?
* **Galatians 1:11–20**: Why is Paul explaining how he learnt the Christian faith? Why is it important to discover things for ourselves? Can we say that we know God for ourselves?

Praying on your own

You may be on your own, but are you aware that God is there with you? Prayer just between you and God is very special.

Praying in a group

Play Chinese whispers, where you pass on a whispered sentence from one person to another. See if it has changed by the end. It's good to have times when we come to God on our own, rather than always hear about God from other people.

Praying it through

Draw your thoughts together in a time of quiet reflection, or use the prayer below.

Here I am, Lord.

❖

NOT THERE YET: PRAYING IN HOPE FOR THE FUTURE

> 'Come and set up your kingdom.'
> MATTHEW 6:10a

INTRODUCTION

We need to remember when we pray that not all our prayers will be answered straight away. Some of our prayers will be answered only in the future. So, wars still happen, and people get sick, and there is unkindness and cruelty in the world, even when we pray. But we go on praying that one day all this will change. And our prayers are like pictures from the future, showing what it will be like.

The psalms are full of prayers for the future, believing that God will bring his kingdom into the world. The prayer Jesus taught his disciples asks for God's kingdom to come. The writers in the New Testament often told us to go on praying and to go on waiting for God's kingdom.

 ## BLOSSOM AND BIRDSEED

Mr Towers was not used to having a garden. He'd lived in the city all his life, in an apartment high above the traffic, the shops and the streams of people walking to the tube station. When he moved to the country, everything changed. He stepped out of his back door and, instead seeing of pavements and newspaper stands, he was surrounded by grass and trees. There was a cold wind blowing, and he thought the garden looked rather dull.

'Something's missing,' he thought to himself. 'I know! Flowers. A garden ought to have flowers.'

He decided to buy some from a catalogue the postman had dropped through his letterbox. There were lots to choose from. Red and orange poppies. Bright blue cornflowers. Yellow and white daisies. Apricot and salmon-pink hollyhocks. Silver flowers, mauve flowers, even brown flowers. The pictures were all beautiful. What a wonderful garden he was going to have!

Mr Towers ticked the boxes on the order form and sent off his money in the post. He also ticked the box for a bird table. It would be fun to watch the birds flock to the table in the morning and to hear them sing.

Days went by, and at last the postman rang Mr Towers' doorbell and handed him two cardboard boxes. One box was very large and had a picture of a bird table on the front. The other box was much smaller.

'Are all the flowers in there?' asked Mr Towers in surprise. 'They'll be squashed.'

He took the boxes into the garden and fetched his trowel from the shed. The smaller box was filled with rows of little packets. Each packet had a wonderful bright picture on the front, all the different flowers he'd ordered. Mr Towers was very puzzled. The packets didn't look big enough for flowers! One by one he opened them, and looked inside.

'Crumbs!' he cried. 'They're full of crumbs! Where are my flowers? They promised me flowers.'

He was so upset he threw all the crumbs on to the grass and crumpled the packets in his fist. A robin came and perched on the garden fence to watch him.

'Just crumbs!' Mr Towers called to him. 'You and your friends can eat them for all I care.'

He tore the wrapping off the bird table, and slotted it together, grumbling to himself. It went wrong of course, and he had to start again. By the time he'd finished and set the table up under a big tree, he was very tired. And it looked as if it was about to rain.

'I think I'll forget about gardening,' he said and went in to watch television.

Weeks went by, and Mr Towers settled into his new home. He bought some paint and painted the ceiling and the walls. He bought some new furniture to go with it. But he never bothered to go into the garden, and he never bothered to feed the birds.

And then one bright, sunny morning, he woke up feeling happier than he had felt for a long time. As he was making breakfast, he heard the birds singing very loudly.

'Dear me,' he thought. 'I don't think I've been feeding them. Sorry, birds.' And he gathered up some pieces of bread on to a plate.

As he opened the back door, a blaze of colour caught his eye. 'What is it?' he cried. 'It's coming from the grass.'

Mr Towers hurried outside. There, growing out of the lawn were hundreds of coloured flowers: poppies and snapdragons, daisies and sweet williams, cornflowers and marigolds.

'My flowers!' he cried in astonishment. 'They must have grown out of the crumbs!'

And he spun round and round in the middle of his wonderful, coloured garden till he felt quite giddy.

PRAYER STEPS

Praying with a visual aid

You will need a fairly simple jigsaw puzzle with the completed picture on the box. On your own or in a group, put the puzzle together. If you are in a group, distribute the pieces around so that each person has a similar number. When you have finished, take time to reflect on or discuss what you have done. Did you find it difficult? Did it help to have the completed picture in front of you? Think how each piece contributed to the end result.

Praying with the Bible

Use the following passages for personal reflection or discussion.

* **Psalm 122:** In what way is this psalm a prayer looking to the future? Is there any point in working for good in this world? Do we pray for peace, and how do we believe God will answer our prayers?
* **Matthew 6:9–13:** Why does this prayer begin with praying for God's kingdom to come? How does this influence the rest of the prayer? How does it influence all our prayers?
* **Jude 20–21:** What is the connection here between praying and waiting? What is the connection between action and waiting? What are we waiting for?

✴ **Revelation 21:3–5:** What is the new order promised in these verses? How is this new order reflected in our times of prayer?

Praying on your own

Take some time to imagine how God wants the world to be. What about your street? Your school? Your local community? See if this helps you pray for your family and friends in a new way.

Praying in a group

Look through some newspaper cuttings and talk about the things that you think aren't as they should be. How do you think God sees them? What do you want him to do? What do you think he wants you to do?

Praying it through

Draw your thoughts together in a time of quiet reflection, or use the appropriate version of the prayer below.

Lord, I pray for your kingdom to come and for the whole world to be as you want it to be. Help me be the way you want me to be. Amen

Lord, we pray for your kingdom to come and for the whole world to be as you want it to be. Help us to be the way you want us to be. Amen

✛

IN JESUS' NAME: PRAYING WHAT GOD WANTS

> **Whatever you say or do should be done in the name of the Lord Jesus.**
> COLOSSIANS 3:17a

INTRODUCTION

Jesus told his disciples to pray 'in his name'. Some Christians today end their prayers with the words 'in the name of Jesus'. These aren't magic words to make the prayer come true. When we pray in Jesus' name, it reminds us that we are joining in with his life and work. Our prayers need to reflect what Jesus wants us to say and do.

In the Old Testament, the name of God is seen as so holy that it is a sin to use it in the wrong way. That could mean swearing or being flippant about God or not saying true things about him. In the Gospels, the disciples were angry that some stranger was doing miracles in the name of Jesus. But Jesus said that the man was doing good work and so they shouldn't stop him.

The name of Jesus is very powerful. Paul tells us that we should live our whole lives in the name of Jesus.

HOST HARBOUR

'Welcome, in the name of Host Harbour Cute and Furry Wildlife Wonderpark,' said the woman, smiling in a very friendly way. 'You can stroke the animals marked green on your leaflet, and you can feed the animals marked yellow. But the animals marked in red will eat you, so please keep your leaflet with you at all times.'

People clutched their leaflets tightly and began to wander along the paths.

'Come on,' said Charlie. 'I'll show you the bears.'

Fergus followed her along a path painted with bear prints leading to a large enclosure surrounded by railings. An attendant stood outside, handing out bear stickers.

'Welcome to the Bear Parlour,' he said. 'Please don't feed the bears. And please don't drop litter. It encourages rats.'

'Don't you want rats?' asked Fergus, who kept a rat at home.

'Host Harbour Wildlife Wonderpark does not classify rats as cute and furry. Please move down the path to the Chinchilla Chalets.'

'It's a bit odd here, isn't it?' whispered Fergus as they patted the head of a baby donkey in the Donkey Dome.

Charlie felt disappointed. 'I thought you'd like it,' she said. 'You're always going on about animals.'

'That's because animals are great. But I'm not sure these people like them.' Fergus frowned. 'Yes, I know. They claim they do everything for the good of animals. But they still keep them in cages.'

'Not cages, young man!' A horrified voice spoke behind them. The donkey attendant had been listening. 'We're not a zoo. The animals are kept in environmentally appropriate luxury confinement zones, for their own comfort and protection. Host Harbour Cute and Furry Wildlife Wonder-park would be very unhappy if anyone went home thinking this was a zoo.'

'It's a zoo,' muttered Fergus as they walked off. 'And what's more, it's a bad one.'

Charlie was beginning to enjoy herself. 'What shall we do?' she asked. 'Shall we let all the animals out?'

'Don't be daft!' said Fergus. 'They'd eat each other. They'd eat you. Then they'd die.'

They came to Monkey Mansions, which were rows of small cages. All the monkeys were sitting huddled on the floor. Their fur was coming out. One was scratching at a sore arm, but otherwise they were doing nothing. They looked tired and bored. The monkey attendant came forward to give him a sticker, and Fergus started to complain.

'These animals are not happy,' he said. 'They haven't got enough space, they're ill, and they don't look fed properly.'

'Host Harbour does everything in the name of animal happiness,' answered the attendant.

'Host Harbour does everything in the name of Host Harbour,' shouted Fergus.

'Sir, everyone else here is enjoying themselves,' said the attendant firmly. 'You can't be expected to know how to look after animals.'

'He does,' said Charlie. 'He's always reading websites and magazines. He belongs to the RSPCA and the World Wildlife Fund and Animal Rescue and…'

'Those monkeys don't look very happy,' said a woman nearby to her husband. 'What do you think?'

The attendant spoke into his radio. Within seconds, two security men in uniform were showing Fergus and Charlie to the gate.

✛

It took them both a long time, but after many letters, emails and phone calls, they were finally told that Host Harbour had been forced to sell up. It was taken over by an agency that did care about animals. Fergus and Charlie were allowed back as special guests.

'In the name of all the animals,' smiled the new manager, 'thank you for your kindness and courage.'

PRAYER STEPS

Praying with a visual aid

Think of someone famous whose work you admire. Write down their name in the centre of a piece of paper. Around the outside, write or draw some of the things you associate with them. It could be their charity work or the country they represent or their great faith or courage or skill. What do you think of when you hear their name? What is it about them you admire? Have they inspired others to do similar things? Take time to reflect or discuss how we associate certain qualities and actions with someone's name.

Praying with the Bible

Use the following passages for personal reflection or discussion.

* **Exodus 20:7**: What do you think is meant by misusing God's name? What are the ways we might misuse the name of Jesus in our prayers?
* **Mark 9:38–41**: Why do the disciples react against someone using the name of Jesus? How does Jesus see the use of his name? Can we think of examples today?
* **Philippians 2:6–11**: What is the status given to the name of Jesus? Why is it given? How does this influence us when we pray 'in Jesus' name'?
* **Colossians 3:17**: How can we apply this one verse fully to our lives?

Praying on your own

Think for a while what sort of prayer Jesus would agree with. End your prayer by using the words 'in the name of Jesus'.

Praying in a group

Discuss what it means to do everything in the name of Jesus—schoolwork, friendships, fun, making choices, spending money. Write a prayer together that you can pray in his name.

Praying it through

Draw your thoughts together in a time of quiet reflection, or use the prayer below.

… *in the name of Jesus. Amen*

BEING THERE:
IN GOD'S PRESENCE

> '**I will be with you always, even until the end of the world.**'
> MATTHEW 28:20b

INTRODUCTION

Sometimes we can think so much about what we are praying, or what is happening around us, that we forget to care whether God is with us or not. The most amazing thing about prayer is that it connects us with the presence of God.

In the Old Testament, Job talked a lot about God to his friends but then was overwhelmed when he found God was there close to him, listening. One of the titles the Bible gives to Jesus is Immanuel, which means 'God is with us'. In the last words of Matthew's Gospel, Jesus promises to be with his disciples to the end. In Laodicea, there was a church who had stopped caring whether God was with them. Jesus told them he was outside the door, waiting for them to open it and let him in.

 ## THE PRINCE'S PARTY

Charlotte was a kitchen maid. She worked in the kitchen of a huge house, so huge that it was more like a castle. Some very important people lived in the house, and they were having a party. Charlotte worked very hard, running around helping the pastry cook to do the baking and the maids to do the cleaning, polishing the knives and forks, and making peanut butter cookies and doughnuts and sausage rolls and strawberry ice cream and fairy cakes.

The very important people who lived in the house were having a birthday party. They had invited hundreds of other people to join them. The most important guest was His Royal Highness Prince Frederick, the king's son. It was his birthday, and he was going to be 21.

The guests began to arrive. Charlotte peeped round the kitchen door and gazed at the beautiful clothes and fancy jewellery and smart suits everyone was wearing. They all looked so wonderful and rather pleased with themselves.

'I wish I could see the prince,' thought Charlotte. She waited till no one was looking and all the guests had arrived and then she crept down the corridor to the ballroom. She slipped inside and hid behind a long, velvet curtain. The whole room was a whirl of colour and sound and sparkling lights. Everyone was dancing or talking loudly or eating the good food. But it was so crowded, she couldn't see the prince at all.

As she hurried back towards the kitchen, Charlotte heard someone knocking on the front door. 'Go away,' the guards were saying. 'We're having a party. The guests are all inside.' But the knocking came again. And again the guards kept saying, 'Go away.'

Charlotte went back to the kitchen, just in time before someone spotted her. She helped to fill the plates with more food. As she carried a huge dish of chocolate mousse over to a waiting footman, she saw out of the window that it had started snowing.

'I love snow!' she cried. Then she heard the knocking again, but this time someone was knocking on the kitchen door.

Charlotte was the nearest, so she lifted the latch and pulled open the heavy door. A young man was standing outside. He was covered in flakes of snow. He had a nice face, but he looked rather angry and upset. 'Will you let me in?' he asked.

'You'll get cold out there,' said the head cook. 'Come in by the fire. Do you want a doughnut?'

The young man sat by the fire, and they saw that he was dressed in very fine clothes.

'Have you come to the party?' asked Charlotte.

'Yes,' he said. 'But they won't let me in.'

'You can stay here,' said the cook. 'We're having some party food in the kitchen.'

So they sat round the table and had a wonderful time, talking and eating and laughing and telling stories. 'Tell us about yourself,' said the scullery boy to the young man. 'Who are you?'

'I'm Prince Frederick,' said the young man. 'And it's my birthday party. All the guests in the other room are having such a good time that they haven't even noticed I'm not there. They've forgotten why they're having the party.'

Charlotte stared and stared. A real live prince sitting at the table with them! And he seemed really glad to be there.

'Well, happy birthday, Your Majesty!' said the head cook. 'We were just going to send in the birthday cake. But it's your cake, so we'll have it here.' And the pastry cook brought forward the biggest chocolate cake that Charlotte had ever seen.

PRAYER STEPS

Praying with a visual aid

For this you will need the kind of plastic windmill you find at garden centres or the seaside. If you are enterprising, you might like to make one. On your own or in a group, take the windmill outdoors or run it around indoors to set the sails turning. What substance is making them turn? Can you see it? Does it seem less powerful or more because it's invisible? How would you know if it wasn't there? Take a while for personal reflection or shared discussion.

Praying with the Bible

Use the following passages for personal reflection or discussion.

* **Job 42:1–6:** What did Job learn about God? How had his faith moved forward? Do *we* hear about God all the time but never really 'see' him for ourselves?
* **Matthew 1:20–25:** In what way was God with us in Jesus? What hope did this bring for the human race?
* **Matthew 28:16–20:** Jesus is about to leave his disciples to go back to heaven. How would they have felt? What does his promise mean? What does it mean for us?
* **Revelation 3:14–22:** What was missing from the Laodicean church? Why was Jesus outside the door and not inside? Have we left Jesus outside our church, however successful it appears?

Praying on your own

Close your eyes and take a moment to think about the fact that you are in God's presence. How does that make you feel? When you pray, remember God is there, listening.

Praying in a group

Sit in a wide circle and close your eyes. Your leader taps someone on the shoulder, and they leave the circle as quietly as possible. Without opening your eyes, see if you can tell who it is. As they return, your leader taps someone else on the shoulder and they have to leave. Again, see if you can tell who it is. Are we aware that God is present with us when we pray? Does it matter if we don't feel his presence with us?

Praying it through

Draw your thoughts together in a time of quiet reflection, or use the appropriate version of the prayer below.

Lord, thank you that you are with me when I pray. Amen

Lord, thank you that you are with us when we pray. Amen

BIBLE INDEX

OLD TESTAMENT

TALES OF GRACE

50 five-minute stories for all-age talks, sermons and assemblies

'Stories help us to see from different angles, they free us to explore our own feelings and beliefs, they engage our emotions as well as our minds, they speak to adults and children alike and they connect us with each other.'

This book contains a wealth of imaginative five-minute stories written with both children and adults in mind. They can be used with only children present, only adults present, or with a mixed-age group and are suitable for use in:

- Church services
- Children's talks
- Family services
- Sunday clubs
- School assemblies
- After-school clubs
- Bedtime or family reading
- Group reflection

The stories illustrate some of the main themes of the Christian life, such as grace, forgiveness, friendship, guidance, trust and prayer. Some have a traditional flavour, others a contemporary setting. Each story is accompanied by sermon pointers for four key Bible passages relating to the theme, questions for young listeners and suggestions for visual aids and actions.

ISBN 978 1 84101 366 4   £7.99
Available from your local Christian bookshop or, in case of difficulty, using the order form on page 173.

ORDER FORM

REF	TITLE	PRICE	QTY	TOTAL
366 4	*Tales of Grace*	£7.99		

POSTAGE AND PACKING CHARGES					Postage and packing:	
order value	UK	Europe	Surface	Air Mail	Donation:	
£7.00 & under	£1.25	£3.00	£3.50	£5.50	**Total enclosed:**	
£7.01–£30.00	£2.25	£5.50	£6.50	£10.00		
Over £30.00	free	prices on request				

Name _____ Account Number _____

Address_____

_____ Postcode _____

Telephone Number _____ Email _____

Payment by: Cheque ❑ Mastercard ❑ Visa ❑ Postal Order ❑ Switch ❑

Credit card no. ❑❑❑❑ ❑❑❑❑ ❑❑❑❑ ❑❑❑❑ Expires ❑❑ ❑❑

Switch card no. ❑❑❑❑❑❑❑❑❑❑❑❑❑❑❑❑❑❑

Issue no. of Switch card ❑❑❑❑ Expires ❑❑ ❑❑

Signature _____ Date _____

All orders must be accompanied by the appropriate payment.

Please send your completed order form to:
BRF, First Floor, Elsfield Hall, 15–17 Elsfield Way, Oxford OX2 8FG
Tel. 01865 319700 / Fax. 01865 319701 Email: enquiries@brf.org.uk

❑ Please send me further information about BRF publications.

Available from your local Christian bookshop.   BRF is a Registered Charity

New Daylight, BRF's popular series of Bible reading notes, is ideal for those looking for a fresh, devotional approach to reading and understanding the Bible. Each issue covers four months of daily Bible reading and reflection with each day offering a Bible passage (text included), helpful comment and a prayer or thought for the day ahead.

Edited by Naomi Starkey, New Daylight is written by a gifted team of contributors including Adrian Plass, David Winter, Gordon Giles, Rachel Boulding, Helen Julian CSF, Margaret Silf, Anne Roberts, Stephen Rand, Tony Horsfall and Veronica Zundel.

NEW DAYLIGHT SUBSCRIPTIONS

❏ I would like to give a gift subscription
    (please complete both name and address sections below)
❏ I would like to take out a subscription myself
    (complete name and address details only once)

This completed coupon should be sent with appropriate payment to BRF. Alternatively, please write to us quoting your name, address, the subscription you would like for either yourself or a friend (with their name and address), the start date and credit card number, expiry date and signature if paying by credit card.

Gift subscription name _____

Gift subscription address _____

_____ Postcode _____

Please send to the above, beginning with the next January/May/September issue: (delete as applicable)

(please tick box)	UK	SURFACE	AIR MAIL
NEW DAYLIGHT	❏ £12.75	❏ £14.10	❏ £16.35
NEW DAYLIGHT 3-year sub	❏ £30.00		

Please complete the payment details below and send your coupon, with appropriate payment to: **BRF, First Floor, Elsfield Hall, 15–17 Elsfield Way, Oxford OX2 8FG**

Your name _____

Your address _____

_____ Postcode _____

Total enclosed £ _____ (cheques should be made payable to 'BRF')

Payment by Cheque ❏ Postal Order ❏ Visa ❏ Mastercard ❏ Switch ❏

Card number: ▢▢▢▢▢▢▢▢▢▢▢▢▢▢▢▢

Expires: ▢▢▢▢ Security code: ▢▢▢ Issue no (Switch): ▢▢▢▢

Signature (essential if paying by credit/Switch card) _____

❏ Please do not send me further information about BRF publications. **BRF is a Registered Charity**

barnabas

Resourcing people to work with 3–11s

in churches and schools

- Articles, features, ideas
- Training and events
- Books and resources
- www.barnabasinchurches.org.uk

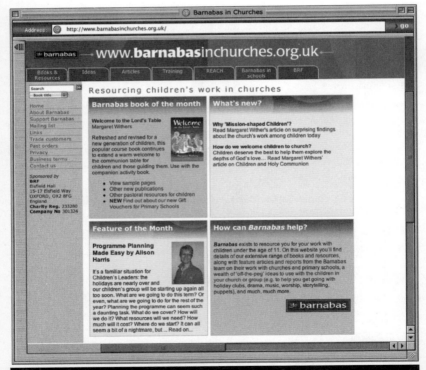